THE DEED WITH THE DUKE

PRAISE FOR SRI SAVITA

"Sri Savita brings heat and tender, lyrical yearning to Regency romance."

— FELICITY NIVEN, AUTHOR OF *THE BED ME BOOKS* AND *THE LOVELOCKS OF LONDON* SERIES

"Lovely, sexy, and deeply kind—*The Deed with the Duke* is a deliciously charming Regency romance. Raaz and Camelia have a permanent place in my heart."

— ALEXANDRA VASTI, *USA TODAY* BESTSELLING AUTHOR OF *NE'ER DUKE WELL*

"*The Deed with the Duke* is a charming historical romance that simmers with sexual tension and deep emotion. Fans of Tessa Dare's *Spindle Cove* and Courtney Milan's *Wedgeford Trials* will gobble this up (along with a plate of raspberry pastries)!"

— KATHERINE GRANT, AWARD-WINNING AUTHOR OF *THE PRESTONS* AND *NORTHFIELD HALL NOVELLAS* SERIES

About the Book

She didn't gamble on love.

SHE HAS THE DEED.

Camelia Parikh is a fallen woman trying to start over. When she wins the deed to a cottage in a card game, she believes her luck has finally changed. A charming coastal village seems like the perfect place to begin again, far from London and her romantic regrets. That is, until the stern Duke of Wednesbury arrives to claim the deed and cottage as his.

HE HAS THE TITLE.

Raaz Panchal, the new Duke of Wednesbury, is searching for the missing deed to his late father's beloved cottage, and he travels to the countryside to investigate. But once there, he learns the home is not vacant, and a beguiling woman claims it's her property now. When her deed proves genuine, Raaz prepares to leave, but then fate collapses the stable roof. Duty to his father's memory—and certainly *not* a pair of alluring amber eyes—compels him to help.

TOGETHER, CAN THEY HAVE IT ALL?

Camelia cautiously accepts the duke's assistance, but between a bold badger, a moonlit waltz, and dangerous late-night wagers, it's impossible to keep her distance from the devastatingly handsome duke. When they surrender to temptation, she can no longer ignore their differences in station or the mistakes of her past, but her traitorous heart already wishes for a future that's surely out of reach.

THE DEED WITH THE DUKE is a steamy, lust-at-first-sight, Regency romance with a grumpy Indian hero, a sunshine Indian heroine, and adorable animal antics. **A detailed list of content notes can be found at the author's website: sri-savita.com/writing**

THE DEED WITH THE DUKE

CARDS OF PASSION
BOOK EIGHT

SRI SAVITA

For readers like me,
who want to see themselves reflected
in the pages of a Regency.

CHAPTER 1

ROBIN HOOD'S BAY, MAY 1817

Robin Hood's Bay welcomed Raaz Panchal with a breeze that carried the sharp scent of the sea up to the cliffs. On this pristine spring day, the sun beamed bright in cloudless blue skies. The wind whipped across the long grass, creating waves that rippled through the blades. Beyond the crooked lines of cottages and narrow alleyways, wildflowers dotted the hillsides with color and sheep grazed over the rolling green in puffs of white like little clouds. The entire halcyon landscape was too perfect. And surely, anything so charming was never to be believed.

Of course, he could understand the appeal of such a hamlet. If one were enamored by both the picturesque and the sublime in equal measure, then yes, the marshy moors, the cliffs, and the sea presented a wonderland. Perhaps that explained why his father had been so fond of the place, though Raaz, his younger brother, and his three younger sisters had never visited before—as obscure and out of the way as it was from their life in London. But his father and mother had loved

1

rusticating at their cottage orné as often as they could when they were newly married.

The deed had gone missing several months ago, but his father died before it could be recovered. So, his was a solitary sojourn in the countryside to regain possession of the deed and bring it back where it belonged—the Wednesbury estate —for both his parents. Raaz had assured his mother he knew it had meant a great deal to his father to have the cottage deed within the Wednesbury estate again, and since the late duke couldn't fulfill his wish before his death, Raaz would honor him by doing it now.

He led his mount, Shandar, up the final stretch of the long, steep hill on which the Wednesbury cottage perched. Raaz had arrived ahead of the hack he'd paid to bring his luggage, but fortunately his steward had managed to track down a spare key, which Raaz now had on his person. Where the original had disappeared to was a mystery, but not one he could solve at the moment. He had a much more concerning problem on his hands right now.

Linens drying on a line outside. A buckskin gelding grazing. Windows open to let the breeze in. Someone, it seemed, had been living here. Possibly for a good while, by the looks of it. Raaz had not expected to find the cottage occupied when he arrived to assess the state of it, but perhaps this was nothing more than a simple misunderstanding. He would explain he was the duke and that this property belonged with the Wednesbury estate. Once he had the deed, he'd send the poor confused chap on his way—with some silver, perhaps, for added persuasion.

With that plan in place, Raaz dismounted and tied Shandar to the hitching post near the fence. He opened the front gate and ventured up the stone path. When he reached the door, he raised his hand and rapped sharply with the W-shaped brass knocker.

After a long pause, the door opened a crack. A voice said, "Sorry. We're not interested in whatever wares you're selling."

"I'm not selling anything," Raaz said. "I'm—"

But he lost his words then, as the door opened all the way. The most beautiful woman Raaz had ever laid eyes on stood before him. Her sable hair cascaded over one shoulder in loose waves. As she swept her hair back with one hand, Raaz followed the line of those long fingers. The delicate skin at her wrist was gold, as warm as the whisky-amber glow in her irises. His eyes followed the natural path of her shoulder upward to assess the curve of her neck. And, despite his best intentions, his gaze dropped to the swell of her breasts as she stepped closer to him.

Raaz sucked in a sharp breath at her sudden nearness. He didn't want to have her so close. He didn't want to catch the scent of her, which he searched for with the ferocity of a hound hunting a fox. Would it be the fragrance of fresh country air? The bright zing of lemons and sunshine? Would she carry with her the clean softness of laundry, or lavender and soap? If he pressed his lips to the hollow of her throat and swiped his tongue there, would she have the sweetness of oranges? The spice of musk?

Goddamned infernal whimsy—it plagued him, pushing him further on the path to fantasy. This woman was a stranger, for heaven's sake—living in *his* house.

He should not want to know what her skin smelled like, much less tasted like.

And yet, he wanted it too much.

The sudden rush of desire surging in his blood shocked Raaz. He reflexively took a step backward to put more space between him and this mystifying woman. Raaz tried to anchor himself to something else. Anything other than the thought of dipping his head to the curve of her shoulder and inhaling the scent of her hair deep into his lungs before grazing her skin

3

with his teeth. His eyes fixed on the nip of her waist. It was then that he was aware of the clothes she wore—a man's shirt altered expressly for her form and buckskin breeches that clung to the curves of her hips and thighs.

It took all his effort to drag his gaze back up to her face, and with a panicked start, he realized that she was studying him, too. She scrutinized him with less subtlety than he did her, raking her intense gaze from his head down to his boots and then back up again. Should he avert his eyes? Raise an eyebrow and ask if he passed muster? Did she like what she saw? Why did he *want* her to? That last question was the one that heated his face.

The charms of women were not lost on him, but she should not have affected him as such. Raaz was not the green lad of his youth. He'd been all over England—traversed the entire continent, in fact. Perhaps it had simply been too long since he'd last been with a woman. This might have been a convincing argument, if not for the stubborn refusal of his memory to furnish a single one of those encounters. He could not remember the last time. Or indeed, any of the times. In that moment, it seemed there was no one he had ever desired. Not like this.

Until now. Until her.

And he didn't even know her name.

Nor was he able to ask, it seemed. Raaz's words tangled on his tongue under her gaze, and for the first time in his four and thirty years, his thoughts staggered to a standstill. He held his breath, waiting for her to say something. Do something.

Finally, she smiled, apparently finished with her assessment. "You'll do."

The words flooded him with a sense of relief that warmed his blood, as if he had been basking in the sun's glow instead of her gaze. He should not care. Who was this stranger in his house, acting like she owned it?

She took him by the wrist and slapped an apple into his palm. "Follow me," she said, withdrawing her touch and leading him into the cottage.

Surely he was addled by the bold contact of her skin against his. Instead of declaring who he was and telling her to leave right then and there, he did follow her inside. They walked through the immaculate front hall, which boasted a large vase of daisies and cornflowers on a round brass-and-rosewood side table, and came to the drawing room.

"Shh." The woman held one slender index finger against her rosy lips before they entered. He kept his footsteps light as they approached the boarded-up hearth. There was a small gap between two loose slats, and out of this opening came a distinct *meow*.

A cat. She wanted his help to rescue her cat.

So why was he holding an apple?

"Here, hold this," he said, giving the apple back to the woman before kneeling at the hearth to investigate.

After a few moments, one golden eye peered out, and then a feline head materialized. The dapper black and white cat looked at Raaz like Raaz was disturbing his home as well as the woman's, and then he strutted out of the hearth as if he were wearing the finest tailcoat. Raaz stood, and the cat circled back. He rubbed against Raaz's legs, weaving between them and purring, then sauntered from the room to find someplace else to nap in peace.

"I knew it." The woman beamed at him. "I could tell Billi would like you."

Why? But he didn't ask her that, because he had no idea why he again cared for her opinion.

She explained anyway. "You seem steady. Observant. Controlled. I think Billi trusts that in a man."

Raaz snorted at the flattery. She apparently trusted him, too, enough to let him in without asking who he was first.

A thought that reminded him—the entire reason he was here was to inform her of who he was. He opened his mouth to speak, but before he could get a single word out, he was interrupted by a bleat from behind him.

He turned back toward the drawing room entrance. Of course. A goat lived in his cottage, too. Considering she had named her cat the Hindi word for *cat*, he took a guess at the creature's name.

"I suppose the apple is for our friend Bakri, then?" Raaz asked in a wry tone, watching her face as they both walked over to the stout black, white, and grey goat. He caught a flash of recognition and surprise in her whisky-amber eyes at the Gujarati word for *goat*.

"Yes," she said. Her relaxed manner returned. "Will you help me lead Bakri back outside to graze?"

So, she was controlled, too. Interesting. Especially when combined with that effervescent optimism.

"Why not?" Raaz drawled. What else were dukes good for?

Once they had coaxed Bakri into the grass, she dusted the apple off on her breeches and reached her hand out to the goat.

"They do better with smaller pieces," Raaz muttered. He pulled out a penknife and handkerchief from his trouser pocket. He unfolded the blade and wiped it on the handkerchief. "Allow me."

She handed him the apple, and he strived to ignore the warmth of her fingers yet again. He sliced off a small piece of the fruit and held it out for the goat.

"Here you are, Bakri. We'll need to find another name for you, though. It's a shame the lady couldn't do any better than *goat*."

"It's a placeholder," she said with a frown, taking the remainder of the apple from Raaz and holding out her other hand for his knife. Something pensive filled her expression.

"I'm told he was quite the troublemaker, and the people trying to rid themselves of him didn't have the decency to give him any name at all. I haven't had much time to become better acquainted with the animals, but it was the least I could do to make sure the poor dear had a name from the start."

And she wouldn't get more time. Because she had to leave, of course.

He was supposed to be telling her that. Right now, in fact.

And yet, he gave her his penknife to slice the rest of the apple for the goat.

"Names are important," he said. Names allowed people to express who they really were, more than titles, more than derogatory monikers like "The Duke of Disgrace" or whatever else the broadsheets came up with for him these days, a consequence of the follies of his youth.

But he wasn't in London right now, so he pushed those thoughts aside.

They both took turns feeding apple slices to Bakri until the fruit was gone, and the goat ambled away, satisfied.

"Thank you," she said, tilting her head and assessing him again. One corner of her mouth tugged into the beginning of a smile. "Who are you?"

"I'm the Duke of Wednesbury." He smiled back. "And you're trespassing on my property."

She studied him. "I don't believe it," she said. She turned and headed back inside the cottage.

"Madam, this is no lark," Raaz said, storming after her.

He followed her to the drawing room again. She took the seat behind the desk and gestured to the chair in front of her —calling Raaz to a meeting in his own drawing room, in his own house.

He raised an eyebrow at her impertinence, but sat in the chair offered to him. He would play her game. For now. And then he would send her on her way. What was a little while more to wait?

"I assure you, I *am* the Duke of Wednesbury," Raaz said again. "And this is *my* cottage."

She kicked her feet up on the desk and flipped his penknife open and closed.

He tried not to focus on the way her buckskin breeches emphasized the shape of her calves that were now crossed in front of him. The sound of the knife opening and closing gave him the distinct feeling that she was deliberately counting out the seconds.

Waiting for a trap to spring.

Only he was the one to be snared. Not her.

A slow smile spread across her face. Something sharp glinted at him in that smile. A hint of a hidden, harder edge, so at odds with the easy charm she had displayed before. He wondered how much of the sunny disposition had been for show.

After all, the warmth of the sun could be dangerous. Presently, under the magnified focus of her gaze, it felt like he was going to burn. The light from her radiant smile was no less lethal.

"No, Your Grace. You misunderstand me," she said at last. "How can I trespass, when I own the deed?"

And there it was. He was caught unaware. Exactly where she wanted him to be.

CHAPTER 2

"I BEG YOUR PARDON," THE MAN SAID GRUFFLY.

"It is you that is trespassing, Your Grace," Camelia said, biting back a smile.

Oh, how it pleased her to disarm a man, and a *duke*, no less. If that was even who he was. Surely this man, who looked to be not much older than her own nine and twenty years and appeared to lack the regular attention of a valet, could not be the true Duke of Wednesbury? Dark whiskers were already visible along the sharp line of his jaw, and it was scarcely past noon. She fought to not let her gaze linger too long on the black cravat at his throat or the warm brown skin that looked like hers. His thick, dark hair looked as though the wind, or his hand, had raked through it. He didn't even have a hat, for heaven's sake.

"Do I have this correct," he said, beginning to tick off the points of his argument on his fingers. Fingers that were long and elegant. Large hands that she imagined might— *No! Stop.* He continued, "You've been living in my house with a cat, and a goat, and your horse, for who knows how long—"

"Ten days," Camelia interjected quickly, but her confidence that he wasn't the proper duke began to crack as his words conveyed the absolute authority—the unmistakable arrogance—that only a duke would be so bold to employ. She willed the heat creeping up her neck to subside.

"—and you let them come *inside*—"

"Pavan, my horse, is *outside*," Camelia corrected. "The goat usually is, too."

"—and now you say I'm the one trespassing," he finished, lifting one brow. Her pride smarted from that cool, dismissive gesture, but she would not give him the satisfaction of hearing her voice quaver.

"The cat I just discovered today," she said, as if that would help his opinion of her. It was perhaps not the strongest of arguments, but it was the truth.

"Lovely," he said, stretching each syllable. "I'm so pleased I could help you with your feline friend."

Camelia should have felt chastised by that low, dark, bone-dry tone. Instead, something tightened in her core. She brought her legs down from the desk in an attempt to create more distance between them, but that did little to help. His long legs invaded the area under the desk—close enough to brush against hers. Camelia's skin felt hot and tight, and her stomach twisted itself into elaborate knots.

"I wonder what else is hiding in the house," the duke said.

His smooth voice conveyed a threat that did nothing to dissuade the fever he inspired in her. His dark eyes were alight with something dangerous. She should have more caution. She should seek some air, posthaste.

"That's none of your concern," she said. "And why, exactly, should I let you, a stranger, prowl through *my* cottage? You haven't shown me any evidence that you are indeed who you say you are."

He snorted. "You first. I'd like to at least have the name of the beguiling stranger who's taken up residence in my cottage orné before you have to leave."

"I'm not going anywhere," she said hotly, crossing her arms in front of her. She would not cower for anyone, even a supposed duke. "In fact, you, sir, should be the one leaving my house, because I was here first."

"Fine," he said, before pulling a gold signet ring from his hand and placing it on the desk. It hit with a distinctive *thunk*. A coat of arms was on its face, and the scripted *W* winked at her in the sunlight slanting through the window.

Camelia's face heated. The engraving matched the door knocker on the cottage. She met his gaze.

"If that doesn't satisfy you," he drawled, "then you may read these." He placed three papers on the desk. "Take as much time as you need. It's not as if I have anything more important to do."

She ignored his insouciance and pored over the documents. The first was a communication between the late Duke of Wednesbury and his son, who was apparently the man seated in front of her now. *Raaz.* She was tempted to speak his name aloud, to test the sound with her lips and tongue.

Camelia swallowed the impulse. The second document contained correspondence between the late duke and his solicitor about this very cottage in Robin Hood's Bay. The third contained notes from the current duke—*Raaz*—and his steward. Evidently, the cottage deed had been lost by the solicitor, and Robin Hood's Bay had been the last place the solicitor visited before Raaz's family lost track of the man and the deed.

Camelia could piece together the rest. The solicitor must have gambled away the deed and lost it to the gentleman she'd won it from in a game of piquet. Or perhaps there had been another owner in between. She wasn't sure how much of her suspicions she should share with the duke, as they wouldn't help him feel better about losing the place. Camelia looked

11

up from the documents to find the duke's intent gaze upon her.

"Forgive me, Your Grace," she said.

He reclined in his chair, folding his hands behind his head.

"But before you get too comfortable here . . ." Camelia let her words trail off as she opened a drawer and produced the deed, along with a bundle of other papers that proved its legitimacy. She smoothed out the folds and slid the stack across the desk to the duke.

The duke pulled a quizzing glass from his jacket and studied the documents with a critical eye. Camelia's cheeks burned, but she had done nothing wrong—this time, at least. It *was* the genuine deed, and she had won it fairly—even if she had been gambling.

She reached for the long, thin gold chain she wore around her neck. It was the only piece of jewelry she carried with her, a birthday gift from her mother when she was younger. Camelia lifted the necklace from under the collar of her shirt to show the key she'd received with the deed, threaded onto the chain for safekeeping. "I also have this."

The duke grunted. "I'll admit it bears a striking resemblance to the one I have." He pulled out another key and raised it next to hers.

As they matched up the outlines, their fingers brushed. Camelia and the duke both drew back, and their gazes tangled together.

The duke cleared his throat. "Well, I stand corrected. My apologies, Miss . . .?"

"Parikh," Camelia replied with a smile.

"Thank you, Miss Parikh," the duke said. "I finally have an answer for where this lost deed landed. It would seem this cottage legally belongs to you."

"So it does," Camelia said, trying not to appear too triumphant.

His keen, dark eyes took in the drawing room, and he looked almost . . . lost. As alone as she'd felt before she arrived here in the Bay. Recognition and empathy sliced through her at the expression on his face as he looked out the window.

"Why are you so interested in this cottage, Your Grace?" Camelia asked. Surely there were other vital matters in London or other properties more worthy of his attention.

"I am not. My father was interested in recovering the deed and preserving this property. It held sentimental value for him." He blinked and tore his gaze away from the window. "But I don't see how that's any concern of yours, and anyway, it doesn't much matter, seeing as how this is now your cottage."

The duke stood, straightened his black cravat, and dusted off his black coat and trousers. "I'll take my leave, madam. I thank you, again, for your help in clearing up my misunderstanding."

"Wait," Camelia said, unable to resist in spite of herself, and he did. "You've come all this way. At least let me give you a tour, Your Grace."

His eyebrows rose, but then the brief flash of surprise disappeared. The duke gave a sharp nod. "Thank you, Miss Parikh. I would like that very much." The hard line of his scowl softened and curved upward into a smile.

And, oh, it warmed Camelia's heart. Which gave her pause.

But no. This was different. This time, she would not be so quick to be taken in by another handsome face. Camelia was only giving the duke a moment of kindness so he could honor his father. It was noble. Once they toured the cottage and the grounds, she would send His Grace on his way. And then, Camelia could keep her new life here—without the danger of an attractive duke around. She'd come to the countryside to escape the regrets of her past in London—and before that,

13

India—and she would keep her promise to herself to avoid temptation.

"Splendid." Camelia rose to her feet and gave the duke what she hoped was a dazzling smile. "Shall we?"

"Please lead the way," the duke said, and he followed her out of the drawing room.

CHAPTER 3

They left the drawing room and walked across the hall to the dining room. From there, they continued the tour to the kitchen, scullery, larder, and storeroom. There was a verandah outside, too, and after making their way to the study and adjoining library, that took care of everything on the ground floor. Then they went down to the beer, wine, and coal cellars.

A coal cellar—in a home with a thatched roof, no less. Why rusticate when you could roast? Raaz shook his head as he looked in at the piles of dark rocks. Only in the country would such a thing stand. London had banned thatched roofs for over a century now. He would have to make sure there were some hearths that burned wood in the cottage. Devil and damn. He rubbed at his sternum, trying to rid himself of the sharp stab of emotion that had made itself known there. It wasn't right. A lady should have a proper home. With a household to help, if it could be managed.

They made their way back upstairs. Somewhere between the verandah and the library, Raaz had realized he could not in good conscience leave yet. First, the thought of returning to

London to face his mother empty-handed, his own grief reflected in her eyes, was too much to bear. Second, he'd noticed very few touches of Miss Parikh's in the rooms. Linens still covered most of the furniture, dust still collected, and boards still closed off hearths. Perhaps she didn't know how to manage a place of this size. If she was amenable, he could offer some suggestions, or even help her tidy and set up the place. He'd leave once she was comfortable, if for no other reason than because he did not wish to see a place his father had cared about fall into disuse and be so uncared for in return.

"And here are the bedchambers," Miss Parikh said after they climbed the stairs to the first floor. "There are five in total."

"More than enough space for you, I imagine," Raaz said, peering down the hallway lined with doors. "You could have a different room for every day of the week, if you so chose, and only have to repeat yourself on weekends."

"Yes, I'll admit that fantasy did make me giddy at first." She blushed, and it tinged her cheeks with a very becoming shade of pink. "But I couldn't justify preparing all the bedrooms when I only needed the one for myself."

"I see," Raaz said, and he followed her while she unlocked each room so that he could have a look inside.

"I chose this one because it's nearest to the closet." She gestured to the two doors at the end of the left side of the hallway. She bit her plump lower lip. "In all honesty, I was expecting something a bit more modest when the gentleman I —ah—acquired the deed from told me it was for a cottage in the country." They halted outside her bedroom door.

"Yes, well, I don't believe the aristocracy quite understands that what is considered *modest* by the rest of the world is something different entirely," Raaz said. "To think my parents spent their time here when they were newly wed with all this space between only the two of them. The upkeep alone is absurd."

He shook his head. "Though I suppose it must've been bliss without five children underfoot."

"Haven't you grown up with more than enough space, Your Grace?" Miss Parikh teased.

"Yes, but I haven't become too accustomed to it, I hope," Raaz said with a scoff. "I'd like to believe I can understand that the rest of the world does not live as we do in the peerage. Besides, I had to share my space with my younger brother and three younger sisters." He grinned. "So I suppose my home did feel more modest with that constraint."

Miss Parikh pushed open the door of her bedroom, and they peeked inside. The visible furnishings included a large bed, a dressing table with a basin for washing, and a cheval glass in the corner, but the rest of the pieces were covered in linens.

There was also a screen behind which Raaz assumed she kept her valise and clothing, and he tried not to let that thought burrow further into his mind.

"I know it's not much," Miss Parikh said. That lovely pink was back in her cheeks. An image of her on that bed, hair mussed and spread out across the pillows—ideally because of him—flashed through his mind.

"Did you spend any time here in the countryside?" Miss Parikh asked.

Darker thoughts replaced his idle fancies, and he returned his gaze to the bedroom. "Unfortunately, no. I never had the chance to see this cottage with my father when I was young. Before he died, I had a conversation with him about how much he missed this cottage. He was upset that he couldn't locate the deed." He turned to face Miss Parikh. "But I am glad to now see this place my parents cherished, so thank you for this tour."

"Of course," she said. "You are very welcome, Your Grace." They walked back down the hall toward the stairs.

"You've truly only been here for ten days?" Raaz asked. "It seems you've accomplished much in that time."

"Yes, it might seem that way," she said, appearing somewhat rueful. "But not quite, no. I'm grateful the cottage was already furnished when I moved in, but as you saw, I've not removed all the coverings yet. I'll admit it was overwhelming to clean and organize the space as one person, and I started working at The Bay Blossom Inn soon after I arrived as well."

"Ah, yes," Raaz said. "I believe I rode past an inn on my way up the hill to the cottage."

"Yes, that's the one."

Raaz supposed it made sense that there would only be one inn in a village as small as the Bay.

"Forgive me for asking such a personal question, but why did you decide to keep the cottage once you saw it?" He wasn't sure why she hadn't tried to get rid of it if the work was too daunting. From the papers they'd traded and read, it seemed like the cottage had changed hands before. Surely she could have found another buyer for a space this large, and for a good price, too.

"I—" She paused and bit her lower lip. "I suppose I wanted something different. And I could not stand the idea of abandoning the place once I'd arrived."

Even if Raaz wished he didn't feel sympathy for her reasoning, he could understand wanting something different. It was one reason he was here in the Bay and not in London right now. Well, all right, that hadn't been entirely his own decision. He was here at the urging of his mother and siblings, who had seen him in the grip of grief over losing his father.

Miss Parikh stopped at the top of the stairs and looked back down the hallway, brow creased. Raaz stopped with her. "Helping Mrs. and Mr. Shroff with the baking and cooking there takes up most of my day," Miss Parikh continued. "Not only for all the guests' meals at the inn, but also because the

Bay is preparing for the summer festival at the start of June. So, I spent some of my nights at The Bay Blossom. The Shroffs, as well as others in the Bay, help me to take care of the animals. But between all that, I haven't had much time."

"I understand," Raaz said, hoping it did not sound like he was passing any sort of judgment. It seemed Miss Parikh was trying to do the best that she could for a single woman of truly modest means. "Though you certainly have enough space to designate a room for the cat and the goat, at the very least. Billi and Bakri may enjoy that immensely."

She smiled at that, and he was glad to see it.

"Preparing the other rooms might also be prudent to give the appearance of another person living here with you, for safety," he said, growing more serious. Someone like a husband. As much as he did not enjoy even the fictional idea of another man making her blush or smile, he liked the thought of her alone and vulnerable to danger even less.

"Your Grace," Miss Parikh said with an impish smile, and she placed a hand over her heart. "The only man I'd have here is you."

At her words, their gazes locked. Miss Parikh's teasing smile faltered, and something sparked to life in the air between them, charging the hallway with a haze of heavy, shimmering heat. Raaz felt the prickle of perspiration on the back of his neck but did not dare move. Or breathe.

He was going to die here, he knew, drowning in the depths of her simmering amber eyes. Left without a single breath of air in this too tight, too hot hall. Or he was going to kiss her. There was no in-between. He needed to do something to break the spell and get hold of his senses, but Miss Parikh spoke first.

"What I mean is, now that I know you're the duke and how much this cottage meant to your father, there's no other man I care to invite for a tour, and I don't have a husband."

Miss Parikh said this with a toss of her hair, as if it were perfectly reasonable to pick up their conversation where it had left off before the heat between them had addled his insides and his brain.

Well, if she remained unmoved, that all but proved she had the powers of a woodland witch, or some wild ethereal sylph. After all, her horse, Pavan, was named for the Gujarati word for wind.

"I understand you're unmarried," Raaz said, and he was glad to have heard his assumption confirmed. "But you could simply lie about being engaged or married. It wouldn't have to be elaborate, and the pretense might offer some security."

The golden light in her eyes dimmed. "I would never lie about matters of the heart," Miss Parikh said, voice small and sad.

Silence followed her admission. Raaz believed she was telling the truth—and that it was a truth not easily given. She guarded her heart. As did he. But no one learned to do that without being hurt before, and Raaz despised the person who had taught her that lesson. It made her darker, and that was his dominion, not hers.

"How did the deed to this cottage land with you?" Raaz asked, attempting to move past the vulnerable moment and thereby spare her any discomfort. "I'd like to believe you didn't steal it." Though she was certainly charming enough to have been successful at such an enterprise.

"Of course I did not steal the deed," Miss Parikh said. "I won it fairly." The pink in her cheeks burned brighter. "In a game of cards."

"Oh?" Raaz exhaled in an amused huff. "Well, then. It gives me great delight to know that, in a place called Robin Hood's Bay, it turns out there is such a thing as honor among thieves."

Finally, she laughed, and Raaz felt the joy of it spread across his face as he smiled, too.

Her expression darkened, as if his answering smile had displeased her.

"What was the game?" Raaz asked, trying to bring the light back to her face.

"Piquet," she said, with obvious pride.

"Well, if someone had to win, then I'm glad it was you and not the gentleman," Raaz said with a grin, and her smile returned.

A part of Raaz wanted to find something else, anything else to say to prolong their conversation. But she turned to the staircase, and they made their way back down the steps to the ground floor.

"Well?" Miss Parikh asked when they were both standing in the front hall again. "Satisfied, Your Grace?"

"Ah, not yet," Raaz said, dragging a hand across the back of his neck. "Shall we take a look at the stables?"

"Certainly," she agreed, and led the way.

Her elusive scent taunted him at every turn—the very essence of summer captured in a bottle. Or perhaps the season was part of her own natural alchemy, and that was why her skin glowed with warmth. As if her touch carried sunshine and anything she grazed her fingers against might also turn to gold.

Though if that were the case, then the cottage would not look so dreary. Unless, of course, it was a fae glamor meant to trick him and keep her treasure safe, and under all the drab furnishings hid true riches and wonder.

Raaz stifled a groan. He was not drawn to whimsy, and so to entertain a tale in his mind for this long was already far too uncharacteristic. Still, it suited her quite well, the lore that she brought the summer season with her to spread throughout the countryside, scattering the rolling green hills with wildflowers to tell the people to rejoice, for the sunlight was here to stay.

Or perhaps she'd escaped from some sylvan wood precisely to plague him. And if that were indeed the case, then he did not want her to disappear into fairy dust. At least not yet. He could not ignore the foolish way his heart leapt at the thought of spending more time with her.

"Here we are, Your Grace," she said, once they'd traversed the short distance to the stables and made their way inside the shaded enclosure. "We'd best get you on your way so that you can make use of the daylight for your journey. I'm sure you'll have matters in Town to return to, and I do think I can manage things myself—"

But her words were cut short as one section of the roof collapsed, and without thinking, Raaz pulled her against him and out of the path of falling debris.

CHAPTER 4

"You were saying," the duke murmured in Camelia's ear.

Even though they stood in the sunshine, a shiver slid down her spine with the heat of his breath. She muttered a curse. The coarse language must have surprised the duke, because he tensed his hold on her.

It was at that moment she realized how close they were to each other.

Camelia shoved him away, which was rather ineffective, as he was a solid wall of muscle and man—broad-shouldered and nearly a head taller than her. The duke didn't move one step.

"I tied Shandar to the hitching post," he said, "and mercifully, your horse and goat weren't inside the stable."

She took a step back, since he apparently wasn't going to. "Yes," she agreed. She barely managed to get the word past the knot of emotion in her throat. What if any of the animals had been inside? She heaved a sigh of relief that no one was injured and sent a silent prayer heavenward.

"Miss Parikh, are you quite well?" The duke dragged his

dark gaze over her from head to toe and back up again. Everywhere his eyes landed, heat radiated through her.

"I'm fine," Camelia assured him. She turned away to assess the state of the stable roof. Once the cloud of dust cleared, Camelia saw the ragged edge where beams and panels had torn themselves away. The break was uneven, and she wondered if the collapse was because the stable was old and needed routine maintenance, or if the wood had been rotting for some time even before she arrived.

"Are you certain you want to manage this mess alone?" The duke's voice behind her was gentle and warm. "If you'll allow it, I could help you—with the repairs to the stable roof, and getting the rest of the cottage in order as well. I'll be here for some time attending to other properties."

Camelia worried her lower lip between her teeth as she considered his offer. Repairing the stable roof was yet one more thing that demanded both time and money. She did not have a surfeit of either.

"I suppose I could consider that," she said, turning back to him. "Thank you, Your Grace."

"I rather think it's time we dispensed with titles, don't you? We've already embraced," he said.

She met his gaze and saw that he was suppressing laughter. In the sunlight, his dark eyes were a warm brown. They danced with mirth—and something else she didn't want to examine too closely.

"How amusing, Your Grace." She rolled her eyes and dusted off her breeches. "I commend you on being able to laugh in the face of danger. Not all dukes arrive armed with a sense of humor, I'm sure, or indeed, such valor."

He chuckled, and the low timbre of it slipped under her skin.

Camelia would not have him teasing her or puffing up with pride that he had saved the poor damsel. She was fine, if a bit shaken. Mostly, she felt out of her depth and foolish. This place was so large, she couldn't possibly take care of everything on her own, and she loathed when she couldn't do things on her own. But she was not so prideful as to neglect practical sense, and she had to do what was best for the animals, too. The fact was, she needed the help, and so it was high time she learned how to ask for it, or at least accept it when it was offered.

"Very well then," Camelia said to the duke. "I agree to your help with the stable and the cottage."

"I'm pleased to hear it," the duke said. "Might we walk to the inn together and discuss our plans further over a meal?"

At his words, her stomach rumbled with hunger she hadn't noticed before.

"Oh, of course," she stammered. "How thoughtless of me. You must be famished from traveling."

"No harm done. I plan to inquire about a room at the inn as well." The duke's eyes twinkled. "And Raaz is fine. Please."

"Raaz," she said, and he did not look away when she said his name. In fact, he smiled—and she did not know what to do with that. It was a hungry smile that told her she'd met someone who could keep up with her. She wasn't sure if the feeling in the pit of her stomach was one of desire, dread, or both.

"You may address me as, simply, Camelia," she said.

"Simply Camelia, it is," he said, and she dropped her gaze because it felt too intimate to watch him form the shape and sound of her name. "Named for the jasmine flower, I presume?"

Startled, she looked up and met his warm brown eyes. "Yes."

"We have some languages in common, I believe," the duke said, this time in Gujarati, and her face flushed again.

She'd registered that the duke could both comprehend and

speak Gujarati and Hindi while they were discussing Billi and Bakri earlier. But the knowledge that they could say things to each other that no one else would understand—well, it was too much to share, and too soon. She couldn't let herself be lured in by this reminder of the home, culture, and languages she'd left behind in India. Camelia didn't even speak anything other than English with Binita and Kabir at the inn, although they were both from India, too.

She started walking down the hill, putting some much-needed distance between her and the duke. "Yes," she replied in English, not wanting to share the intimacy of speaking in her native language with him. At least, not yet. Her attraction to the duke would be too dangerous for her heart. But she appreciated that he was offering some semblance of genuine connection to help her feel at ease with him, and so she did not want to be rude.

She had not expected the duke to have an interest in flora. Doubtless he spent his time among the more fashionable and fast set in London, not among the people and plants in the countryside. "Do you study botany, Raaz?"

"I would not call myself a botanist by any formal training," the duke said, falling into step beside her. "But it is a keen hobby. Plants help me learn a place. To distinguish between them on my travels, I've often kept journals with notes and sketches." He shrugged. "It keeps the mind busy and entertained."

No doubt there were other temptations that would keep a duke busy and entertained, but Camelia found it endearing that a man who looked like the very definition of a rogue would instead pass the hours by studying plants and making meticulous notes and drawings in his journal.

"I also enjoy artistic endeavors," she said. Though she'd brought her art supplies with her to the Bay, she had less time for them now than when she'd worked as a finishing governess. "Painting, most especially."

"And what do you like to paint?" Raaz asked.

Camelia was surprised by his interest. No one had ever asked her about her painting preferences before, and it had been so long since she had picked up her brushes that she couldn't say for certain. "Portraits, I suppose. They're what I like best. The way you appreciate learning from plants, I appreciate learning from people."

She felt his gaze on her as they walked, studying her exactly as she'd just said she liked to study a person.

"That's not to say I don't enjoy capturing a landscape," she said, turning to the duke when she could no longer resist the temptation to look at him. "And the Bay does offer a bounty of beautiful vistas for that."

"Hmm. Yes," Raaz said. "Lovely, indeed."

And he did not take his eyes from her face.

Camelia stumbled over her own boots and had to avert her gaze to pay attention to the path they were taking down the hill. "Have you ever been to India, Raaz?"

"No, I haven't. My siblings and I were born and brought up in England, as were my parents, though they've tried to preserve the traditions of their parents and pass those along to us," Raaz said. "Where did you reside before arriving in the Bay, Camelia?"

"In London," Camelia said. "Before that, in India."

"And when did you arrive in England?"

"When I was nineteen. I came to look for work," she said. "I was a finishing governess in London before coming to the Bay."

She was saved from having to answer any more questions about herself for the time being by their arrival at The Bay Blossom Inn. She knocked, and Binita opened the door.

"Camelia, dear, what a sight for sore eyes you are," the proprietress of the inn said. "But isn't this your day off?"

"Yes, it is," Camelia said. "But I'd finished the washing and then—"

"Oh my," Binita interjected with a gasp. She turned to her husband, who had arrived to greet them as well. "Kabir, he's the new Duke of Wednesbury. His Grace looks exactly like his father."

"Your Grace, please accept our condolences," Kabir said. "We were so saddened to hear of your father's passing. We used to see the late duke and his duchess often when they were first married."

"Ah, yes, my mother told me they greatly enjoyed spending their summers here in the Bay," Raaz said.

"The late duke and his duchess married around the same time we did," Binita explained to Camelia. "We had just opened the inn when they came to the cottage that first summer and stayed for the festival."

"That's lovely," Camelia said.

Raaz glanced at Camelia. "Several months ago, of course, the deed was lost, and apparently the cottage as well."

"And now I have both," Camelia said, turning to Binita and Kabir.

"Well, isn't that a wonder," Kabir said.

"Indeed," Binita said. Her gaze darted between Camelia and Raaz.

"His Grace is interested in a room here," Camelia said quickly.

"Yes," Raaz confirmed, just as fast. "A hack should be arriving with my trunks either today or tomorrow. Earlier, a portion of the stable roof at the cottage collapsed—"

"Goodness, that sounds like a fright," Binita interrupted. Her brows knit together with concern.

"We're all fine," Camelia assured her and Kabir. "Including the animals."

"That's a relief," Kabir said.

"Yes, thank heavens for that," Binita agreed.

"I'm hoping to stay here at The Bay Blossom while I help Miss Parikh manage the repairs," Raaz said. "I'll be here for a while, as I have other properties in the Bay to visit, as well as the tenant farms."

"Not a problem, Your Grace." Kabir said. "We're happy to have you as our guest, and we will help in any way we can."

"Thank you. I appreciate that, Mr. Shroff," Raaz said. "I'll need to find men who can assist with the roof repair."

"Of course, Your Grace," Binita said. "Why don't you both have a seat. No doubt you must be hungry."

"Thank you, Mrs. Shroff," Raaz said.

"Binita will do just fine, Your Grace," the older woman said with a smile.

"And you must call me Kabir," her husband added.

"Very well, Binita and Kabir. Then I insist you call me Raaz," he said.

"Of course, Your Grace," Binita said with a nod, quite obviously flustered that he would forgo formality so soon. "That is, Raaz." She dashed off, presumably to check on the food.

Kabir smiled. "I'll see what I can do about finding men to help you, Your Grace—ah, Raaz."

"Thank you," Raaz said with a chuckle.

Kabir turned to Camelia. "As for you, beta, you must also take a room here at the inn until it's safe to walk about the cottage."

Ignoring Camelia's weak protests, Kabir led them to a table inside. Binita returned soon after with plates of bread and cheese, lemon cream, pound cake, and cups of masala chai. Camelia and Raaz ate and drank in comfortable silence.

Camelia tried not to focus on the shape of his mouth, but that proved more difficult than simply telling herself not to look. He had quite a distractingly handsome face.

"What is it? Do I have something on me?" Raaz asked, when he caught her staring. He scrubbed a hand down his face. "Damn and blast. Evidently, I forgot to shave this morning."

She laughed. "You also forgot a hat."

"So I did," he said, laughing too.

It felt like something bigger than themselves had brought them together to revive this cottage, and Camelia was committed to seeing the work through. She could keep her attraction to him separate from their work. If her body still remembered how, without hesitation, he had banded his arms around her to protect her from the collapsing stable roof—well, that did not matter. If she could still feel the warmth of his chest, what of it? She would teach herself to forget. It was a lesson she had mastered before, and it was far too soon to let her heart get away from her head—with a *duke* of all people. She would avoid setting her sights on dreams too grand for her. She'd tried, once, to reach above her station. It hadn't ended well. She would not make the same mistake again with another man. His would not be the first pretty face from London she'd had to forget, and she promised herself that this time, she would not fall in love too fast.

CHAPTER 5

FORTUNATELY, THE WEATHER IN THE BAY cooperated, and Raaz was pleased with how much progress they'd made in one week. Thanks to the men that Kabir rounded up to volunteer and some of the tenants, they managed to repair a great deal of the damage to the section of roof that had collapsed. Raaz and Camelia helped prune the overgrowth in the gardens as well. The ivy, woodbine, and climbing roses had been tidied up, too, around the entire building. On the whole, the cottage was a solid structure, and now, from the outside at least, it seemed restored to its former splendor, shining like a place fit for a storybook fairy tale to begin.

Today, after breakfast at The Bay Blossom, Camelia and Raaz walked to the cottage to take care of the animals and to start sprucing up the interior. They'd decided to begin with the bedrooms. After they'd hauled several ornate carpets outside, Raaz took a broom to the first of the bedrooms on the left side of the hallway, and Camelia started on the last of the bedrooms on the right side. He hoped he'd be more focused this way, working separately from her. Unfortunately, it was all too easy to slip into thoughts of her as he swept the floor of the bedroom.

Already it had proven difficult to resist the desire to kiss her amid the backdrop of pink and yellow climbing roses, or really anywhere in this bloody picturesque Bay. And that was just the monumental effort required during the bright light of day, when there were people around to keep his urges in line as they worked side by side in the sunshine. But at night? Under the cover of darkness, his needs turned wickedly carnal. He tossed and turned in his bed at the inn, knowing that only one thin wall separated her from him, wondering if she lay in her bed thinking of him as well.

It was too much to bear, so he'd decided to keep his distance, for now. He was here to help her, not take advantage of her. Raaz did not want Camelia to think he was simply interested in her because she owned the cottage that once belonged to his family. She'd not expressed any interest in him that indicated attraction, and perhaps that was best so as not to complicate their temporary professional arrangement. Besides, he needed his focus for his other errands in the Bay. They represented only a fraction of his new responsibilities as duke, a title that brought with it the tangled thoughts and emotions his father's sudden passing had left him with. He sighed and, for a moment, let his forehead rest against the broom handle.

Of course Raaz had known he'd inherit the Wednesbury title one day, but even at four and thirty, *one day* had still felt far off. It was naive, perhaps, but no less true. Raaz had been shocked, and the loss still hurt. It helped to be away from London for a bit, especially in this village, where he had a piece of his father to connect with that seemed special and separate from the other memories. He enjoyed seeing the village and imagining looking through the eyes of a younger version of his father.

Falling back into the monotony of dusting and sweeping, Raaz appreciated how the labor of cleaning and moving furniture could keep his darker thoughts at bay. Once he'd finished with the two unoccupied bedrooms on the left side of the hall, Raaz headed downstairs to the ground floor. He'd just reached the last step when a shriek made his blood run cold.

Camelia.

He took the stairs two at a time, trying to remember which bedroom he'd last seen her enter. But she was already in the hall when he reached the top of the stairs.

"What is it?" Raaz hurried to her, surveying her for any sign of harm.

"I'm fine," she said, but he could see she was trembling.

"Camelia," Raaz said, pulling her close. "Please. Tell me."

"I don't know what it is," she said into his chest in a nervous rush. "And it wasn't here the last time we looked through the rooms together."

He still had no idea what she was talking about. "I want to help, love, but I need a little more information than that. What wasn't here before?"

"I was cleaning the room across the hall from mine, and I heard"—she hesitated in a way that did not reassure Raaz—"a noise."

"Well, go downstairs," Raaz said, pulling away and rolling up his shirtsleeves. "And let me deal with this sound."

"It's possible that it's more of a situation than a single sound," Camelia said with a weak laugh. "And I'm not going anywhere. What if *you* need help?"

Raaz sighed and pinched the bridge of his nose. "Fine, but at least stay behind me."

They approached the bedroom door.

"What exactly am I going to find behind this door, Camelia?" Raaz asked again.

"I don't know the full extent of what it is," she hissed. "Because I ran out of the room instead of waiting to find out."

"Then kindly allow me, and stay back," Raaz commanded. "Preferably where you can make a clear and fast escape downstairs without taking a tumble in the process."

Truth be told, he didn't want to get injured, either, but he certainly couldn't allow her to investigate.

"Don't hurt yourself, either," she warned, as if she had read his thoughts.

He ignored her words and only held out his hand for the set of keys she carried. Camelia placed the one that would open the bedroom in his palm, and he steadied his breath. He inserted the key, turned it by small degrees, and opened the door only an inch so that he could peer into the room. Still nothing. So he cracked the door open another inch, praying that it didn't make a noise.

And dash it all. The door creaked.

A low, rumbling snarl ripped through the room, followed by a shrill screech.

That was enough for Raaz. Before the thing could snap its teeth, he slammed the door shut and turned the key in the lock.

"We need to leave," he said, grabbing Camelia's hand lest she try to debate him. "Now."

He raced through the hallway and down the stairs. He did not stop until they were both outside the cottage and the front door was locked, too. Side by side, they stared at the door, breathing heavily.

"Your Grace," Camelia said, glancing up at him and yanking her hand from his grasp. "To be very frank, your face has gone pale, and it's quite disturbing."

He raked a hand through his hair. "Listen to me. The first thing we are going to do is find something to eat." He'd worked up an appetite moving furniture. Raaz might need a stiff drink, too, but he didn't mention that part. No reason for Camelia to see him rattled if she was already alarmed.

"The second thing we are going to do," he continued, "is find someone to help evict the infernal creature that has taken up residence in that room."

"What exactly *is* in that room?" Camelia asked.

Raaz exhaled a harsh breath and faced her. He tried to keep his voice even to avoid causing her panic, though he was cursing the recklessness with which she had taken up residence in this deuced cottage alone.

"There's a badger curled up on the bed, as cozy as a damned lapdog," Raaz said. "*That* is what's in there."

"A badger?" Camelia paled, too, and turned toward him.

"Yes," Raaz confirmed.

"Well, it wasn't here before," Camelia said, crossing her arms. "Where did it come from?"

"How in the blazes should I know?" Raaz growled. "Maybe it managed to sneak in when we had to deal with Bakri getting tangled in the Aubusson rugs I was hanging on the fence rails."

"You say that as though it's my fault."

"I told you to close the front door before you helped me beat the carpets."

"Well, if you noticed the front door was open, Your Grace," Camelia shot back, "then why didn't you close it?"

"Well, because—" Raaz started, but he had no argument for that. "Fine. Forget how it got inside for the moment. First, we need to determine how to get it out. Now, do you have any arguments against abandoning the cottage in favor of the inn for the time being?"

Camelia sniffed. "No," she said. "I believe that's best."

"I'm beyond elated," Raaz replied, not bothering to hide his sarcasm as he led the way down the hill to The Bay Blossom Inn.

~

CAMELIA AND THE DUKE OF WEDNESBURY DID NOT exchange two words to each other for the entire trek down the hill to the inn. Her cheeks heated with shame as she walked. Even when she tried her best, she still somehow managed to look like a fool, despite her most valiant attempts to prove that she could, indeed, handle things alone.

"Oh, don't fret, my dear," Binita said, after they'd arrived and been promptly escorted to a table. Binita had misread the reason for Camelia's maudlin mood as she and the duke ate their meals in silence. "This occurs from time to time. It's nothing to shed tears over. Happens to the best of us in the Bay."

"Animals routinely crawl into the cottages?" Camelia asked, sinking her teeth into her lower lip. What had she been thinking by deciding to turn over a new leaf here?

"No, no," Kabir chimed in, joining them. "Only Basil, thank heavens. And you've found him now, so we're all fortunate for that."

"Basil?" Camelia said, just as Raaz said, "It has a *name*?"

"If you took any extra fruit home after we were done baking the past few days, that might have drawn him to you," Binita said with a laugh.

"We'll be sure to check the perimeter of the cottage for any tunnels that might lead back to Basil's sett," Kabir assured them.

"But, you know," Binita said, "denizens of the Bay believe it's good luck when Basil visits your home."

"I wouldn't say he was visiting so much as invading," Raaz said. "Perhaps even commandeering. He certainly sent us retreating. What do the stories say about that? If there's no protocol in place, then I've half a mind to start collecting rent."

"Don't let the mighty beast scare you, Your Grace." Kabir chuckled. "His growl is worse than his bite."

"I'll have to take your word for it," the duke said wryly.

"Well, join us, and you'll find out," Kabir said. "Together we'll relocate Basil to the outdoors. I'm going to see who else I can gather." He left the inn, presumably to round up a few more men at the neighboring tavern, and Binita bustled away to attend to another patron.

"I was unaware dukes were trained on how to herd badgers," Camelia scoffed.

"Standard education at Eton," the duke quipped, "believe it or not." He was staring at the door that had just swung shut behind Kabir.

"Raaz," she said. "What on earth are you thinking of doing?"

At the change in her tone, he turned to her, excitement burning in those intense dark eyes.

"I haven't the faintest idea," he said, "but it seems like it might be fun."

"And dangerous," she added.

"That, too. An added incentive," he said. He, unlike her, sounded thrilled by the challenge. "It's been a long time since I've enjoyed a bit of fun, and there's no way in hell I'm going to stay behind while the other men battle with the mighty beast of the Bay."

"No one's battling the badger, Your Grace," Camelia said. "They're simply rescuing Basil from the cottage."

"There, you see?" Raaz said. "Not so dangerous after all, now is it?"

Kabir came back inside, followed by several other men.

"And besides, there will be other men with me," Raaz added, gesturing at the group as they approached Raaz and Camelia's table. "The only reason I ran out of there with you

37

was because I didn't want you in harm's way. I'm not concerned about myself in the slightest."

To Camelia's dismay, she realized in that moment that *she* was concerned about him. Very much. What if it wasn't Basil but some other badger, and this one was rabid, and then she'd be responsible for getting the new Duke of Wednesbury injured?

"Worry not," Kabir said. "We'll bring His Grace back to you in one piece."

Her gaze flew to Raaz's. Dark eyes glimmering with mirth, he lifted one brow in a sardonic challenge, as if to ask, *Will that finally satisfy you?* Insufferable man. The duke did not need her permission, and he knew that. So Camelia turned away from the duke and muttered to Kabir. "Oh, he's not mine to return."

"Indeed, I'm free to do as I please," Raaz said. He turned to Kabir as well. "So, if I die nobly, and you bring me back in a hundred pieces, please have the lady store them all in Basil's room to remember me by. There'll still be more than enough space in that accursed cottage."

And though his droll words weren't meant to be a battle cry, all the men still cheered.

CHAPTER 6

DESPITE HIS BRAVADO AT THE INN, THE RELOCATION of Basil was straightforward, a simple matter of luring the creature away from the cottage with fruit and honey and shutting the door behind it. However, Raaz enjoyed how the modest adventure brought him closer to the men of the hamlet. With Basil safely out of the way, Camelia moved back in, but for most of the following week, Raaz and Camelia didn't have much time together. The rain made it difficult to accomplish any work outdoors for several days, and Raaz needed the time to visit the other buildings and properties in the Bay that were part of the Wednesbury estate. When it was drier, Raaz and Camelia cleaned out the bedchamber that Basil had taken up residence in.

When Raaz showed up to the cottage with dark circles under his eyes midweek, Camelia insisted he move his trunks from the inn to one of the rooms in the cottage to reduce at least some of his travel. As dangerous as Raaz felt this was for his mental fortitude, it only made sense if he was to keep helping her while attending to his other duties, so he gratefully accepted.

He was spared much temptation, however, for Camelia was busy at The Bay Blossom helping Binita with festival preparations, as well as an increased number of guests at the inn. The two women also left The Bay Blossom in Kabir's care for a few days while they traveled to neighboring villages. They needed to stop at markets and purchase ingredients for recipes to test before the fast-approaching annual festival that marked the start of summer in the Bay. The sixth day of June would arrive in no time.

After the hectic sennight, Raaz encouraged Binita and Kabir to host an assembly at the inn on the first day of June, to give everyone in the village a chance to celebrate all the hard work on the stable roof repairs and festival preparations. He didn't want the couple to feel overburdened, so he paid for every expense to make sure the village had all the food and drink they wanted without Binita, Kabir, or Camelia needing to cook, prepare, or buy anything. Raaz's only condition was that the three of them promise not to tell anyone outright that this was his idea or that he had funded the assembly.

When Raaz entered the inn on the evening of the first day of June, he saw that his efforts had been worth it. The Bay Blossom looked transformed, as elegant as any Mayfair ball or country estate house party, while still maintaining the quaint charm that was all its own and characteristic of the village. There were pink and yellow roses from the cottage to decorate the place, as well as flowers in vivid violet hues from the village garden behind the inn. Mirrored girandoles were mounted on the walls, and crystal candlesticks were placed in clusters on the tables around the perimeter of the floor. The prisms scattered the candlelight across the room to spectacular effect, and colors danced on the walls. Camelia and Binita had decorated the floor with white-chalked rangoli and other designs depicting the very flowers placed around the room.

It seemed as though everyone he'd met in the Bay was in

attendance and already well into celebrating. Raaz was more than ready to finally have that drink he'd promised himself after helping Kabir and the other men relocate Basil to the fields. And, he had to admit, he was very much looking forward to seeing Camelia again. He searched the crowded room for her face.

"Good evening, Your Grace," she said, materializing next to him in a swish of bright amaranthine silk skirts, with the thin gold chain she always wore around her neck on full display. The cottage key wasn't on it tonight.

Despite all the color and beauty in the room, she captivated him the most. Her heavy, dark hair was pulled back into a soft, low chignon instead of her typical three-strand plait. A few loose tendrils had already escaped their pins to frame her face. The hairstyle exposed the long column of her throat to him. His greedy eyes swallowed up the sight of her bared bronze skin, and when they reached the low neckline of her bodice, the swells of her breasts rising above the lush, vibrant silk tempted him to touch and taste.

"Good evening, Miss Parikh," Raaz said, summoning the effort to train his gaze on her rich amber irises—though, to be sure, her eyes were no less stunning than the rest of her. He was as dazed by seeing her in a gown as he'd been the first time he saw her in breeches.

The two of them took their drinks and found a secluded table in the corner. A group of men at a nearby table was telling tales about their bravery with the badger. Then Binita began playing a lively melody on the pianoforte as everyone helped compose an ode.

"Old Basil reigned mighty in the house on the hill," Kabir started.

"Until the day a duke arrived with unmatched skill," someone else sang.

41

Binita picked up the next line. "He battled the great beast of the Bay—"

"All I did was open a door," Raaz shouted.

"And may the Duke of Wednesbury live a hundred years more," the men shouted back in unison.

"God, I hope not," Raaz said, before taking a very large swig of his ale. The songs about Basil's rescue grew more and more mythical.

He couldn't remember the last time he'd smiled this much in the midst of a crowd—with so many people that already felt like friends. Still, the mantle of attention wasn't something he could ever wear with natural ease, and so after a few more verses about the badger rescue, he stood to help move tables and chairs to the edge of the room.

Binita attempted to organize everyone into some sort of country dance that the hamlet was rehearsing to open the summer festival on the sixth of June. Raaz's eyes darted to Camelia, then to the inn's exit that was now blocked by pairs of people.

Binita joined him. "You are more than welcome to join us, Your Grace," she said, keeping her voice low enough that no one else could overhear. "Please."

He met the older woman's gaze, and though Raaz humbly wanted to beg off and escape to the cottage, he found he couldn't do it. This was his village to look after now, and he did not want to disappoint Binita, Kabir, or any of the other people who made their home in the Bay—Camelia included. She seemed comfortable here, and it was obvious she cared so much for these people already.

"I can't imagine she wants you to stand here staring at her, Raaz," Binita said. "Ask her to dance."

He hadn't realized his gaze had drifted to Camelia, and he quickly turned to Binita with a scowl. "No one needs to see

42

that. It's been ages since I've attended a ball, and I'd rather spare her feet the pain."

"This isn't Mayfair, Your Grace. There's no need to be afraid," Binita countered.

He bristled at the insinuation that he was a coward, but she simply raised one eyebrow, daring him to challenge her. Well then. She wasn't entirely wrong, he supposed.

"No one from the beau monde is here to spout scandal," Binita said, prodding him again. "The most we'll do is add another verse to our lyrical legend about a badger, and where's the harm in that?"

"As long as we don't immortalize him as King Basil," Raaz said with a wry smile. "Can't have the beast outranking me in the history books."

Binita smiled. "So, you'll stay?"

"One dance," Raaz agreed, scrubbing a hand down his face. "But not a minute more," he warned.

She beamed at him, then all but shoved him in Camelia's direction. As he made his way through the throng of revelers, Raaz was struck by a sudden sharp stab of emotion. He rubbed at the spot on his chest to ease the tightness, unsure why he was so overcome.

Perhaps it was because Binita reminded him so much of his mother. Or because he was happy to be in this village that had meant so much to his father. Maybe it was the fact that each time Camelia's face lit up at a couple whirling across the floor, he felt the same light of longing for her. Or because, against all reason, Raaz was starting to like the Bay—this lovely, absurd, incredible place—with all its warm people, and its wily badger, too.

"I CAN'T," CAMELIA SAID, LAUGHING, AS BINITA tried to convince her to dance one more set. "I must rest my feet."

The warm press of Raaz's palm against her back reassured Camelia that he wasn't far behind as they exited the circle of dancing people. They'd danced so many times that she'd long lost count. Despite his repeated apologies for not attending as many Mayfair balls as he should have, the duke was a skilled dancer. It had taken Camelia one week of watching everyone rehearse the sequences of the summer festival country dances and reels before she had learned the steps enough to perform passably well. With his impressive athletic grace, Raaz made it look easy and learned all the steps in only a few turns.

Raaz guided Camelia toward an empty table, but Camelia shook her head. They'd already taken a break in between sets to eat and drink, and now what she wanted most was to feel the night breeze on her skin.

"Some air, then?" he murmured near her ear, and she nodded, trying to ignore how the low, rich velvet of his voice threatened to steal what little breath remained in her lungs.

Raaz took her hand and led her outside to the courtyard behind the inn. Camelia held her skirts with her free hand as he guided her along the rolled gravel paths and past a babbling fountain. Rows of crocuses, lilacs, and rambling sweetbriar roses in shades of purple bordered the neatly trimmed topiaries and hedges, and vines wrapped around the legs of stone benches in trellised alcoves. She and Raaz walked under a pergola draped in lush ivy and found a bench hidden from view. They sat down, and Camelia tilted her head to the heavens, letting the cool air kiss her face and throat.

The moon shone bright, and she marveled at the cloudless sky above. Out here in the countryside, it was easy to find and name each individual star that winked down—something she'd never been able to see in the sky above London. The only sounds that kept her and Raaz company were the rustling of grass and the chirping of insects. For the first time in many months, Camelia felt truly still. A sense of peace washed over her with every deep lungful of night air that she took.

Raaz stretched his long legs out in front of him and angled toward her on the bench. Her skirts brushed against the dark blue leg of his trousers. The fabric looked almost black by moonlight. He wore a matching jacket and a dashing deep green silk Jacquard waistcoat with an intricate gold floral design. His muslin shirt and cravat were white. As Camelia studied him, she realized she had never seen him without the black cravat that showed he was mourning his father—until tonight.

"If we were in London tonight, I'd ask you to waltz," he said.

"Even if we're not in a ballroom, you can still ask, Your Grace," Camelia teased.

"I suppose I can." The corner of Raaz's mouth tugged into a smile. "And what would you say?"

"That's cheating, Duke," Camelia said with a laugh. "You won't get an answer out of me unless you ask."

"As you wish, Miss Parikh," he said, standing and holding out his hand. "Waltz with me."

"Now really, Raaz, that's more of a command than a question," she said. "Try again, and please, call me Camelia."

He dropped his hand to his side, but that one side of his mouth kicked up into another smile, and it sent a jolt to her chest. "Camelia," he said.

A furious fever spread through her like wildfire when she heard her name in his voice again after hardly any time together recently. She tried to fight it to no avail. Seeing his lips form the shape of each sound, hearing it fall from his mouth in that lush, low voice—well, it was enough to sear the moment into her fantasies forever. As her pulse quickened,

Camelia realized that, somehow, she had started to desire his rare smiles. Already she eagerly wondered how else she might coax one from him. She craved the familiar comfort of them—of *him*. The warmth of his attention made her weak, and yet all the while, she craved more. But it was too much, too soon. It would be wiser to have more caution.

"Camelia?" Raaz said again.

"Yes?" she said, keeping her voice bright so he would not suspect something was wrong.

"Will you honor me with a dance?" He studied her face before holding out his palm once more.

"Yes," she said again, putting her hand in his.

She was letting him get close enough to hurt her, she knew. But it was inevitable. She *would* be hurt. Eventually, the duke would leave for London, and she had no desire to return there. To say nothing of the fact that he would need to marry a woman of English nobility. As a fallen woman trying to leave her past in the city behind for a new home in the countryside, Camelia was the furthest thing from a lady of the aristocracy. She'd never make a suitable wife for a duke, let alone a model duchess. There was no avoiding the pain of their separation when the time came. But that was a problem in her future and not in her present.

So, when the duke pulled her to him, she did not resist. When he hummed near her ear so they would not be without music, she laid her head against him to feel the sound of his voice and to listen to his heartbeat. Camelia closed her eyes and inhaled his scent of oranges, almond, and bergamot. There, too, was the faint undercurrent of comforting, warm leather, perhaps from cleaning Shandar's tack. She let herself sink further into this moment, and she made a fervent wish that this waltz would remain in her memory. Because at least she could keep that, if not him, forever.

CHAPTER 7

It felt like Raaz only had Camelia to himself for a few minutes before the door to the inn banged open, and she sprang away from him with a start.

"Shh," he murmured to soothe her panic. He drew her into his arms again. Then he turned them both so that her back was pressed against one of the stone courtyard walls, and they were both hidden in the shadows.

Camelia's amber eyes met his, and the force of that single look was staggering. Her irises shimmered in the shadows, as if the luminescent moon was now forever preserved in the heat of her gaze. There was lust there and longing. Raaz felt it, too. Silvery moonbeams cast a shine over her dark hair, and he wanted to take down her pins, tangle his fingers in her tresses, and see if he could catch the rays of light.

"What is it?" she asked, tipping her face up to him as he bent closer to her. They were standing so near to each other, almost sharing the same breath, that she practically pressed the question to his lips.

He swallowed, and her eyes caught the motion before darting to his mouth.

"Raaz," she said, and he felt another surge of lust at the sound of his name in her low, intimate murmur. He leaned forward and nuzzled the delicate spot where the line of her jaw met the soft lobe of her ear, and he was rewarded with the satisfaction of making her breath hitch. "We can't."

"Can't what?" he whispered against her throat.

"Whatever this is," she said, and her words were all breath. "Whatever's making you look at me that way."

He grazed his teeth against the shell of Camelia's ear, drawing another sharp breath from her.

"Why?" he said, smiling against her neck. "Do you want me to stop?"

"No," she answered, and her quick response was a relief. "But someone might see us."

"No one's here," he murmured. "And I promise I'll protect you."

But he spoke too soon. Muffled giggles and whispers floated toward them on the breeze, and the sound of footsteps in the courtyard came closer. Clearly, others had the same idea to sneak away for a moment of privacy in the moonlight. Raaz didn't bother to hide his frustration and growled into Camelia's hair. Lemon and lavender filled his senses. There was something else, too, something distinctly floral but too subtle to name, and he pressed closer to her, hunting it.

She laughed at his muttered oath and raked her fingers through his hair. "I did warn you."

"So you did," he said with a sigh. Raaz pulled away from her, and the sudden burst of cool air made her shiver. He shrugged out of his jacket and wrapped it around her shoulders.

"Thank you." She held his jacket closed with one hand and interlaced her fingers with his other hand.

"Come," he said. "Let me take you home."

∼

THEIR WALK TO THE COTTAGE PASSED IN EASY silence. But much as Camelia tried to appear placid, inside she was a tangle of heated nerves. It had taken everything in her to tell Raaz to stop, especially when he looked like he wanted to devour her right there against the courtyard wall.

By the time they were back inside the cottage, she regretted having had the sense to resist surrendering to the pleasure the duke would have willingly given her.

"Here we are," Raaz said, and his voice drew her from her woolgathering. They had stopped in the hallway outside her bedroom. Raaz rested one shoulder against the wall to the side of her door.

"Here we are," she said.

Raaz raised his brows and huffed a laugh.

"I suppose we should get some rest," Camelia said.

"Yes, I suppose we should." Yet the duke did not move to leave, only leaned against the wall. Waiting.

Fine. If he wasn't going to make this easy on her, then there was no reason she had to make it less difficult for him.

"I will see you in the morning, then, Your Grace." She unlocked the latch to her bedroom door. Raaz caught her wrist, and she hid her smile before turning to face him. "Yes?"

"I only wanted to wish you a good night," he murmured, lifting her hand to his lips. He kept his eyes on hers as he placed a kiss on her knuckles. "I hope you have the loveliest dreams."

Then he moved his lips to the inside of her wrist, and Camelia's heart thudded in anticipation. But he promptly dropped her hand before she could feel his lips catch her pulse there. She bit back a curse. So, this absolute devil of a beast was playing with her. Well, she would simply have to do the same.

Camelia made her voice as sweet as honey. "I hope you have a lovely night as well."

"I will," he said. Obvious amusement glimmered in his dark eyes, and Camelia ignored his mirth as she opened the door to her room one single inch.

"On the other hand," Raaz drawled. "What if there's another lurking animal resident you missed, or heaven forbid, the roof caves in here, too? For the sake of your safety, I should check this room again."

"Perhaps you should," Camelia challenged, and opened the door wide.

"Perhaps I will." He followed her inside. "And perhaps I'll stay. For my own peace of mind."

"Fine. Do as you will," Camelia said with a wave. "But if you seek peace, go elsewhere. Because I have no intention of sleeping at all tonight. Or staying quiet."

"Oh, is that so?" Raaz purred, and she realized the lascivious bent to her words too late. "How remarkably wicked of you."

"Not in the slightest," she dismissed, trying to grasp at the last shred of her composure as she struggled to light a candle. "Fancy a game of cards?"

"With you, clever minx?" Raaz gave a dark laugh. He dragged his gaze down the length of her body and back up, and Camelia felt like she was on fire from the heat in his stare. "That is a tempting offer."

"Well, Duke?" Camelia snatched her lucky deck from her bedside table. She took a seat on one of two sofas around a low table and began to shuffle while she waited for his answer.

"I know I should refuse and will almost certainly regret this later," Raaz said, sitting on the second sofa across from her, "but I want to witness your talent in action. You managed to win the deed to my cottage. One only wonders if you'll charm your way into a more impressive prize this time."

Well, Camelia wouldn't let *one* get away with such obvious innuendo. She arched a brow, then flicked her gaze down to his lap and back up to his face. That did the trick to wipe away his smirk.

"It's a matter of skill, not wiles," she said, affecting boredom, "and if it will help to soothe your pride, then you may choose the game, Your Grace."

"Vingt-et-un," he answered without hesitation. He leaned over the low table to whisper in her ear. "But remember, my darling vixen, you asked for this. And when you won the cottage, you weren't playing against me."

CHAPTER 8

IN THE END, IT WAS UNSURPRISING SHE TROUNCED him so thoroughly. He sat across from her, in perfect view of her bed, and Raaz had a deuced time trying to focus on the cards instead of envisioning the things they could do together there. Even here, on one of the sofas. Or on the low table between them. He could lay Camelia down, get on his knees and— Well, that specific delight may be a more difficult maneuver given his height, but he would bloody well manage it if that's what she desired. Raaz didn't care where. All he knew was that he had to have her.

"Just remember you asked for this," she taunted, throwing his own words back to him.

She was deliciously smug, and victory made her radiant. It lit up her eyes and her smile. In truth, he wasn't quite sure he had lost, not if it meant he could see her this incandescent with joy. It was a prize to be coveted, and if this was how it felt to lose, then he would happily surrender to her each and every time.

"I deserve that," he admitted, once she was done gloating. "So what will you claim?"

Her smile faded with the dawning realization. "We didn't set a wager."

"No," he said, and draped one arm over the back of his sofa. He tried to appear languorous to avoid showing his delight. "We did not."

"What now, then?" She chewed on her lower lip, and he wished she would play fair for once. It took all his restraint not to leap up and soothe the spot she bit with his tongue.

"I suppose there are two options," he said with a shrug, trying not to linger too long on the way the moonlight from the window slanted across her skin. "You can let me choose the prize, or we can play again."

She narrowed her eyes. "You may choose the prize."

He saw that she was not entirely without suspicion. He would have to proceed with caution to make sure she was comfortable.

"I hoped you'd say that," he said. This time his words were not laced with sinful promise. He kept them warm, instead of wicked.

"Why?" she said, apparently assessing him. "What exactly do you have in mind?"

"A kiss." He searched her face to see how his suggestion would be received, not daring to so much as breathe.

She angled her head, studying him with those sharp, bright amber eyes—as though a fox might, or a cat, perhaps. It was like that first day he had fallen into her thrall, when she took his penknife and laid her trap.

And like he had then, he waited for her move.

Finally, she asked, "Do you kiss me, or do I kiss you?"

Her curiosity did not convey any coy artifice, and the direct question—equal parts bold and innocent—surprised a laugh from him.

"Ideally," he said, biting back his smile, "it's best if we're both equally invested in the venture."

"Yes, thank you. I assumed as much." She rolled her eyes. "But who begins the effort, Your Grace?"

"As it's your prize, whomever you prefer," he said.

She paused to consider, and Raaz felt like time stopped entirely. He'd never deliberated kissing at such length before with a woman. It seemed to prolong the anticipation, something he didn't altogether despise with her. It was pleasing to simply be in Camelia's company. Even if he was hard as granite the entire time. He would endure it. For her.

"I'll do it," she finally said. She stood, walked over to his side of the table, took hold of his jaw, and tilted his gaze up to meet hers.

Now *this* was promising. He regarded her with a raised brow but said nothing, wanting to see what she would do next —because she wanted to, not because he willed it. Raaz appreciated a certain degree of assertiveness in all things, but especially when it came to bedsport, and he didn't want Camelia to participate unless it was equal and enthusiastic on her side, too.

"Second thoughts?" he asked, and pretended to nip at her thumb. "It's not too late to put an end to this. Just say the word, and we'll stop."

"Never," she said.

And then her lips met his.

IT WAS THE LIGHTEST, BRIEFEST OF TOUCHES, AS SHE was afraid of desiring more. Still, she could not resist *wanting*. So, she held his face between both hands, relishing in the sensation of the dark stubble along his jaw. Camelia kissed the left corner of his mouth, and then the right, before pulling back. She hadn't studied him from this close yet, and this was her chance to look as much as she wanted. His dark eyes caught the candlelight, drawing her nearer to him. She traced the line of his jaw with one finger, dragging it down to linger for a single moment at the pulse in his throat.

"There," Camelia said, before quickly withdrawing her touch. She did not trust herself to say more. The air was too thin now, like he had stolen her breath with a kiss *she* gave.

"No, darling." Raaz laughed without scorn—in a way that heated her blood. The sound was soft, but a warning all the same. "That was not a kiss."

One of his large, warm hands curled around the nape of her neck, coming to rest under her hair, and his other arm snaked around her waist. He didn't even have to pull her onto his lap—she went willingly, letting herself be drawn into the circle of his arms.

"Fine," she breathed. "Then show me."

Maybe now she would take something from him, too.

"Ah, but you only had to ask," he murmured. With those confounding words, he pressed his lips to hers, as if speaking this way were clearer. He gently bit her lower lip, slipping his tongue inside when she opened for him. It made her mind go hazy around the edges with heady lust and desire. He tasted her, with slow, syrupy kisses that threatened to pull her under.

When Camelia swayed, Raaz's hands slid down her hips. He gripped the rounded curves of her bottom and pulled her nearer to him. Even with her skirts, she could feel every inch of him. Camelia pressed closer to the hard heat of his erection, aligning his thick length with where she wanted him most, and ground against him for more pressure. Everywhere their bodies touched, sparks ignited and licked through her veins. Liquid arousal pulsed between her legs from the delicious friction. She gasped, trying to draw in more air, but what escaped was a moan. Raaz kissed down her neck, lightly grazing his teeth over her flushed, sensitive skin and across the tops of her breasts above the neckline of her bodice.

"God, you feel divine, Camelia," Raaz said through his own ragged breaths. "Don't be shy. Take what you need. Use me as hard as you want to, love."

She tugged one hand through his hair and spread her fingers as she skimmed her other palm down his back, trying to hold as much of him as she could at one time. Raaz responded by dragging his hands along her back, too. They were both frantic in their movements, rubbing and clawing like feral creatures, a climbing tangle of limbs, as if they wanted to crawl inside the other.

And then Raaz pulled back. All of a sudden, it was over.

"What's wrong?" Camelia asked, fearing she had done something he didn't like.

"Nothing," he said, grazing her lower lip with his thumb, and it thrilled her to see his breaths were as broken as hers. "But I don't want to spend without at least having been inside you first."

"I see," she somehow managed to say, even as it felt like she was burning from the inside out.

A slow, wolfish smile spread across his face, and then he leaned in to whisper. "I'd say I won that round. Wouldn't you?"

"Again," she said. Because he was right. "We should do it once more."

What she had given him had not been a kiss. Those four letters were not enough to contain what *this* was now. It was wilder and more expansive. Something that grew and branched between them. Something that could be dangerous and all-consuming if they let it have its way. No, *kiss* was too small—too tame—a word for how it felt. For how much she felt even now when their lips were no longer touching.

"Yes, I'm sure one kiss isn't enough for you—"

"I meant another game," she interjected, before he could tease her any further.

"I think not," he said with a laugh. "You've damned near killed me already. It's late, and I need to meet with the tenant farmers in the morning. So our little deal of desires, or game of pleasure, or whatever this is, will have to resume tomorrow."

"And will it?" she asked, trying not to sound too eager.

Raaz studied her for a moment. "If you want it to continue, then yes."

Camelia took a moment to think, and she appreciated that he did not rush her decision.

Were she to pursue such a path of pleasure with the duke, it would be a dangerous game—this desire deal, as he called it. She knew he would not stay in the Bay forever. His duties in London and elsewhere within the Wednesbury estate would demand his presence eventually, and besides, they could never marry. A ruined woman did not make for a proper duchess, she was not part of the nobility, and she had no desire to leave her new life in the Bay to return to London. But perhaps she could use the limitations her mind provided as a way to protect her heart from falling in too deep with Raaz.

"I do want it to continue," she said, trying to find the best words to express herself. "But I think we should only indulge this attraction for as long as it takes to finish the remaining work on the cottage."

"With any luck, and if the weather eases the way, then we should finish the stable roof repairs in about another week." Raaz's expression was unreadable.

Camelia nodded. "After that, it's best that we end this arrangement, as it cannot lead to anything more between us. You have to return to London. My life is here in the Bay. You're the Duke of Wednesbury. I'm obviously not a member of the aristocracy. So it's better if we focus only on the bedsport and leave the rest out of it. I'd much rather avoid any painful parting or regret when the time comes."

Camelia did not want to risk darkening her memories of their enjoyable time together here, so it was wisest to not form any expectations of a more serious commitment between them. She'd already been burned twice in the past by the falsely glimmering hope of love, and Raaz's station would not allow him to promise her anything more permanent than temporary physical pleasure anyway. It was important she remember that from the beginning—and voice it aloud for both of them, to make it crystal clear—before they surrendered to lust and temptation. She waited for Raaz to say something, hoping that he both understood and accepted this arrangement.

He stiffened slightly underneath her. Some emotion flickered across his features, but it was gone again before she could identify it. "One week of physical pleasure," Raaz said, fixing his intent gaze on her. "Nothing more and nothing less."

"Yes," Camelia said. "That is what I'm proposing."

"Then I agree to your terms, Camelia. But take heed. Next time we play this game, I will show no mercy," he said, with a dark, delicious hint of roughness in his tone.

"I look forward to it," she said, smiling. Neither would she. She wanted to make the most of the time they had together.

She slid off his lap and straightened her skirts, then walked behind the screen that was off to one side of the room. She changed out of her gown, stays, petticoat, and stockings and left on only her chemise. Camelia draped her clothes over the screen. When she stepped out in front of the duke, she was satisfied to see Raaz's gaze catch on the bared skin of her legs and drag over her shift before jumping back up to her face.

A muscle ticked in his jaw, and his throat bobbed as he swallowed.

Well, it served him right for cutting their intimate interlude short. Let him suffer for a little while longer.

"There's a Chesterfield in the library," he said. The words were satisfyingly hoarse. "I can sleep there."

"Your Grace," Camelia teased, "you do remember that you have your own room here at the cottage?"

"Indeed," Raaz said, shifting in his seat. "But something tells me I'll need to sleep farther away from you tonight than across the hall."

His eyes followed her as she walked to the bed. Good. She hoped that meant she could convince him to stay the night in this room. With her.

"There are sofas here, too," Camelia said, pulling down one corner of the counterpane. "But I'd feel safer if you were in my bed."

"Would you indeed?" Raaz laughed. "I'm not certain I could say the same of myself."

Yet he stood and walked behind the screen.

Camelia sat on the bed and listened to the sounds of the duke kicking off his top boots and changing out of his clothing. Her throat went dry as she watched him lay his clothes near hers over the screen, and she swallowed, willing herself to maintain her steadiness. She was so close to winning yet another game between them tonight.

When he emerged—in only his shirt—Camelia struggled to keep the heat that suffused her skin from addling her thoughts, too.

"And you promise to behave?" Raaz asked, voice warm with amusement. He paused near the candle.

"You are the one who wishes to wake early, Duke," Camelia said, turning away to hide her smile. "Not I."

He snuffed out the flame, and Camelia lay down, satisfied with her victory.

"Very well then." Raaz blew out a long breath and muttered a curse before sliding under the covers beside her.

"What is it?" she asked.

"I believe I will have to thank that blasted badger," Raaz said with a sigh. "Perhaps Basil does bring good luck to the places he visits, after all."

Camelia turned her face into her pillow to smother her laugh.

CHAPTER 9

Before the sun was fully up, Raaz had risen and so had his cock. The raven silk of Camelia's hair tickled his face, and he allowed himself one more moment to fill his lungs with the lavender and lemon fragrance of her. That out-of-reach note that escaped him still made him wild. Trying not to wake her, he carefully extricated himself from the warm tangle of their entwined limbs. Somehow, during the course of the night, he'd wrapped himself around Camelia so tightly that his already aching appendage was nestled in between the perfectly rounded curves of her arse.

Don't get too comfortable there, he scolded his erection, and himself, before leaving her bed in search of his banyan. Then he went to his room to find a change of clothes from his portmanteau. A douse in cold water before a brisk ride to meet with the tenant farmers ought to help distract him from the temptation to take himself in hand and seize some small scrap of relief. Raaz was stronger than the damned demands of his stubborn arousal, and he would not come again before he fucked Camelia. Before he gave her pleasure in all the ways he could. Until he was completely spent—his sweat in the sheets, and his seed inside her.

It was this last bit that snapped him out of his fantasy, even more than the cold water he washed with, because that could never be. Raaz had to exercise more caution. If he did spill inside Camelia, then it could lead to a child—something neither of them were prepared for. She wanted a week of mutually satisfying their physical needs, and that was all. A casual arrangement between them.

She was right, of course. He would have to leave the Bay for London eventually. He understood her reasons, and he accepted her terms. It was exactly what he would have offered had he been the one to suggest the idea first. But somehow, hearing it from her had him wishing for more rain, or for another badger to invade the cottage. Anything to give them more time together.

Before saddling Shandar to visit the tenant farms, Raaz checked on the cat, the goat, and Camelia's horse, to make sure they, too, had their breakfast.

CAMELIA WOKE WITH THE SUNLIGHT STREAMING IN from the window and caressing her cheek, but when she reached across the bed, it was cold and empty. She sat up and rubbed the sleep from her eyes. Her gaze drifted to the bedside table, but there was no note.

She swung her legs over the side of the bed and almost tripped. Apparently, Camelia had tugged the entire counterpane around herself during the course of the night. It fell in a crumpled heap to the floor. She turned back to look at the bed and frowned. There was a neatly folded quilt at the foot of his side.

That was assuming, of course, that she could declare it his side already. The duke had collected the deck of cards they'd played with the night before and tucked them back into the box on her bedside table.

She hoped the duke would continue to spend the night with her in this bed as part of their arrangement, and not his separate chamber across the hall. But she hadn't insisted on that as a condition last night. She supposed it was possible that Raaz might want his privacy during the week on occasion. Camelia might too. Perhaps that would help even more to maintain the distance needed between them and ensure they could end this arrangement with no hurt feelings.

She squared her shoulders as she left the room, along with all thoughts of Wednesbury within its walls, and prepared for another day of work at The Bay Blossom Inn. After washing up, Camelia donned a long-sleeved morning walking dress of fine Indian sprigged muslin with a light silk pelisse in prim-rose. She wove her hair into two long plaits and pinned them into a coronet before wrapping a matching primrose dupatta around her head and tying the two ends together. It would keep her hair out of her face while she was baking. She checked her reflection in the cheval glass that stood in one corner of her room. The finished effect was more attractive than a straw bonnet, to be sure, but still, Camelia wished she could have secured the length of silk around her hair with one of her mother's Indian jeweled brooches instead.

She patted the long, thin gold chain around her neck, thankful to at least have the necklace with her here in England. Her lucky deck of cards had also been a gift from her mother, and the treasured items comforted her even though she'd had to leave both her parents behind in India.

She finished her ensemble by tugging on her kid-leather half boots. Her first task was to check on the animals.

When she stepped outside, Billi's black and white body and tail wove between Camelia's legs, and the cat purred with obvious contentment. It wasn't the sharp meow of hunger the feline usually greeted her with, which was surprising. She spotted a small dish on the ground that had been licked clean.

"It seems the duke already gave you breakfast," she murmured, scratching behind the cat's velvet-soft ears. When she checked on the rest of the animals and discovered that Raaz had already tended to Bakri and Pavan's needs as well, her heart warmed, even though she was supposed to be leaving that particular part of herself out of any thoughts about the duke.

Camelia decided to let Pavan stay behind at the cottage to graze. She wanted more time to sort through her heated recollection of last night on the walk to The Bay Blossom.

There was the dance. And the kiss, of course. But there was also the way he had found her warmth when she'd stolen the blanket. The duke might only have been that close to Camelia to block out the chill, but the evidence of his ardor was at her back all night, and she had wanted to press against him and claim her own satisfaction again. One kiss had not been enough.

But there would be time enough for pleasure tonight.

As she neared the inn, Camelia dragged her thoughts back to her surroundings. It was a clear and beautiful day in the Bay, and she basked in the warmth of the spring breeze beckoning the heat of summer closer, the music of the waves crashing against the rocky cliffs, and the colors of the green hills bursting with wildflowers.

"Good morning, dear," Binita said brightly when she entered The Bay Blossom.

"Good morning," Camelia replied, though it took quite a bit of mental effort simply to form those two words.

Binita studied Camelia for a few long moments. "Everything all right?"

"Yes. Merely thinking about all there is to do before the festival." Camelia turned away from Binita to straighten the chairs at the tables around the dining room. She wasn't sure how convincing she was, but her claim was plausible considering the sixth day of June was only a handful of days away.

Thankfully, Binita did not ask her any further questions. The two women passed the time working side by side in comfortable silence. The tarts and breads they made were both challenging and enjoyable, and Camelia appreciated that avoiding idle hands also made it difficult to dwell on her night with the duke, or wishes for what might happen next. She'd promised her help with the festival, and she wasn't going to disappoint Binita, Kabir, or the rest of the Bay.

"Don't look now, but I see your shadow is here," Binita said, startling Camelia from her thoughts.

"Finally decided to grace us with his presence, did he?" Camelia murmured wryly, and the older woman laughed. Inside, Camelia's heart gave a violent thud. How had the hours passed so quickly?

"You wicked thing," Binita said. Her eyes sparkled with mirth. "You mustn't tease the duke."

"Wednesbury won't do anything to me," Camelia scoffed. *Not unless I ask.* Out of the corner of her eye, she watched the duke walk in and sit down with two other men. A shiver ran through her at the thought of all she could ask him to do with her in her bed.

Camelia turned her attention to the men speaking with the duke. She did not immediately recognize them, so they must not be from the Bay. This village was small, and by now she had learned who most of the residents were. The men carried themselves with a level of self-assurance that only came with being among the ranks of the peerage. Camelia did not want to disturb the duke if he did not want to acknowledge her first, so she resisted the urge to walk over to their table and ask if the three men needed anything to eat or drink. Instead, she busied herself with attending to the other visitors gradually filling up the inn.

CHAPTER 10

"WHAT IN THE BLAZES ARE YOU TWO DOING HERE?" Raaz said with a laugh, dropping into a chair at the rickety wooden table that Leo and Percy were seated around.

"Come now, Duke, do be cordial," Percy said good-naturedly. His dark hair had flopped over his green eyes, and he raked it back with one hand. "Prashant and Aarav mentioned you were here, and we wanted to see with our own eyes how the new duke was surviving."

"Honestly, Wednesday, is that any way to treat your friends who've come here all the way from London?" Leo added, raising his arms and stretching, as languid as a cat in the sun.

"Will you give it a rest with that bloody nickname?" Raaz muttered dryly. He rolled his eyes. "And I didn't ask you to leave the comfort of your townhomes to travel to the country."

"Word around the Bay is that you fought a badger," Leo said. His hazel eyes shone bright with mirth. "As two of your closest friends, we weren't going to miss the chance to hear the tale from you firsthand."

Raaz tugged at his cravat to loosen it while his friends stared at him. Waiting.

"Well?" Percy asked.

"Well, what?" Raaz grunted. He searched the room for someone who might be able to shove his friends full of food or drink so they'd cease asking him to talk about himself. He did not want to bother Camelia, of course, but surely Binita or someone else was around somewhere. Although at the moment, it seemed that everyone was busy.

"Tell us about the blasted badger," Leo said. "And don't think you can avoid spending time with us while we're here, either."

Raaz rolled his eyes before obliging his friends and recounting the events. He hoped that they wouldn't leave with only tales of the most ridiculous things Raaz had done in the Bay. He was here to honor his father . . . and escape Town for a bit. But it seemed Raaz could no longer take cover in the blissful obscurity of the Bay. His friends brought London's shadow with them, and it loomed large and dark in his mind.

"There. I've told you all about my tussle with Basil," Raaz said, leaning back in his chair and crossing his arms. He hoped he appeared more at ease than he felt.

Leo and Percy wore matching satisfied grins. "Wait until your family hears of this. Rohan will need to find a badger of his own just to keep pace with you," Leo said.

Raaz stiffened, waiting for the familiar punch of grief to his gut. Rohan was managing the household while Raaz was in the Bay, and Leo's comment was another reminder of the consequences of his father's death.

But it was a softer prod this time—as if the space around the grief had, somehow, expanded to make room for it. To hold it, support him, and keep his memories safe. He was here, not in London. It was not that horrific night, and he was—well, certainly not fine, of course. But *it* was fine. At least in this moment, he was all right. Raaz could allow himself to hold his grief the way it held him. *Gently.* He could let it wash over him without gripping him, without him fighting with it.

He did not resist it.

And he could breathe. So he did, exhaling a breath he'd unknowingly kept trapped in his chest.

His father was woven into his time in London, but also his weeks spent here in the Bay. He should feel the same pain . . . shouldn't he? And yet, there was no vise that closed around his heart. No rising anxiety about needing to stay one step ahead of the darkness. No sharp stab of emotion behind his sternum that he had to force back down before the tide threatened to pull him under.

Perhaps it was because he didn't have direct memories with his father in the Bay, only stories of how much the late duke had loved the cottage and spent summers here with Raaz's mother. Or perhaps it was simply the nature of this place. The Bay was helping and healing him in a way that London never could.

Perhaps it was because she was here, too.

His eyes drifted across the room to Camelia. Her plaits—two today—were wound under a dupatta. Even in practicality, she was lovely.

The clearing of a throat jolted him, and he returned his attention to his friends, who were in the process of exchanging a glance.

Raaz frowned. "Tell me, what's the real reason you two unbridled libertines are here in a small, sleepy village like the Bay? Doubtless, London is more your speed, and you can't have exhausted every attraction in Town already."

"Oh, even London amusements grow tiresome eventually," Leo said, surveying the crowd at the inn. Raaz did not like the way his friend's appreciative gaze took on an altogether rakish gleam when it drifted to where Camelia worked behind the counter.

"Besides, even the fastest among the beau monde will soon be flocking to the countryside for the summer," Percy added, "and Leo and I wish to sample the charming delights this little Bay offers before all of Mayfair descends like vultures."

"I see," Raaz said. "And what exactly do you plan to do here?"

"Why, take in the fresh air, of course, and bathe in the sea," Percy said. "I've heard it strengthens the constitution—healing, relaxing, fortifying, and bracing all at once."

"I fear you put too much faith in miracles, my friend," Raaz said. "Our Bay may not be mighty enough to reverse the effect of all the cheroots you've smoked and spirits you've consumed."

"Nonetheless, we shall try," Percy said, with a dangerous smile.

Raaz had the sneaking suspicion that the path from the shore all the way up to the rocky cliffs would be lined with ladies hoping to catch a glimpse of his friends swimming in the waves.

"Yes, exactly," Leo said. "Mind you, Duke, we're not the ones tangling with badgers in your village, so don't look at us like we're creating trouble for you."

"Not trouble, precisely," Raaz acquiesced. His friends were, at the heart, good people. "Mischief, more like."

The London papers and broadsheets had gifted Leo and Percy with almost mythical status as two of the "Lords of Mischief," and of all the places on earth they could unleash their havoc, the Bay was not one that Raaz would have thought to find them.

"My, my, well, that's certainly a rather more diplomatic way of putting it," Leo said. "With a silver tongue like that, Raaz, you'll be ready for the House of Lords in no time."

Raaz tensed and pressed his lips into a firm line. He was reminded of Camelia's words from last night. He could not escape London forever. He had an entire dukedom outside of the Bay to manage, and those duties would draw him back by the start of next Season. Icy dread pooled in his gut.

"Always so surly and severe," Percy chided.

"Don't forget secluded and secretive," Leo added.

"We're here in the Bay because we want to make sure you're well, that's all," Percy said with a lift of one shoulder.

His expression was so sincere that Raaz had to look away.

"There are many who want you to succeed," Leo added, "your friends included."

Raaz dismissed the sentimental statement with a wave, but he had to admit it was nice to see his friends. He hadn't realized how much he missed the people who made London feel bearable. Perhaps that's because the Bay was starting to feel more like home now. But Raaz pushed that thought aside.

Leo and Percy detailed what Raaz had missed since he left Town for the Bay, and Raaz listened and laughed even as his mind wandered to Camelia. He slid a surreptitious glance to the counter, but she was preoccupied with baking preparations. Raaz tried to ignore the sting to his pride produced by his not attracting her notice. She was here to *work*. And maybe she did not want to interrupt his reunion with his friends? Yes, that must be it. She was being kind. Naturally. Although it was perhaps for the best that she did not cross paths with Leo and Percy. There was no need for her to learn about the carousing of his past. Though, considering she had won the deed to his cottage in a gaming den, she might have actually enjoyed spending time with his reprobate friends. He did not much relish the image of Camelia lining up to watch Leo and Percy dive into the Bay. Raaz frowned.

"What are you glowering about now?" Leo asked him.

"Nothing," Raaz said vaguely, rubbing at the back of his neck. "I'm thinking."

"About?" Percy probed, at the same time that Leo said, "Well, don't hurt yourself."

"The land bordering the cottage," Raaz said, answering Percy's question and ignoring Leo. "I've some ideas for building there."

The words were out before Raaz had time to consider them fully. He hadn't broached the conversation with Camelia yet. He felt the stirrings of a kind of excitement he had not felt before. It would be a challenge, of course, and he was no architect. But it would also provide a way for him to contribute to a place that had meant so much to his parents. Perhaps, later, he could revisit the properties and buildings in the Bay that were part of the Wednesbury estate and see if any of those could use improvements, too.

That he might have more time with Camelia in the Bay was no small part of his motivation to pursue these enterprises, of course. Raaz knew that.

But that did not mean these efforts were any less worthy of his time.

"Do you, now?" Leo asked with apparent interest. "And why might that be?"

But Raaz was barely paying attention. He wasn't even looking at his friends. Binita had said something that made Camelia laugh, and the sparkling sound captured his entire focus.

No one else in the room existed, and Raaz was only aware of her.

He'd had little opportunity to observe Camelia like this—from outside her orbit, not in direct conversation or contact with her. He was transfixed. It was like watching the sun. Best not to do it directly, of course. It was safer that way. But still, he was helpless to resist following her light.

". . . Raaz?" Percy's voice came to him as if from a distance.

At his name, he turned to his friends and blinked out of his daze. "Hmm?"

"I said, who is she, Raaz?"

"I've watched your gaze dart to her no less than one hundred times during the course of this entire conversation," Leo said with a snort. "Do not insult me by denying it, Wednesbury."

Damn Leo. He was too sharp for his own good, and it did no service to Raaz, either. "Congratulations are in order then. I wasn't aware you could count that high, old friend."

"Thank you. How fortunate for me that you're easily impressed," Leo deadpanned. "Being the son of a wealthy duke, I've never had cause to count anything, so I'll allow this insult to stand." He tipped his head in Camelia's direction and grinned. "Provided that you introduce us to your lovely friend."

"She's busy," Raaz said, as he watched her press fresh raspberries into a tart. "I think it's best if we don't distract her."

"Doubtless you believe your hesitation to be chivalrous, so I'll do you the courtesy of not calling you a coward—"

"Somehow, remarkably, I believe you just did," Raaz interjected.

"—but rather come to your aid by ordering food and drink to ensure we're not wasting her time," Leo finished, ignoring Raaz's comment.

"We'll support business in the Bay simultaneously," Percy added.

"And we'll take rooms at the inn. We might as well stay through the festival," Leo said, pointing to one of the signs on the wall of the inn. "We'll even wait like perfect gentlemen until she has a break in customers. Any other arguments?"

"No," Raaz said with a sigh.

"Good," Leo said.

"Now, while we wait, will you tell us who she is?" Percy asked again.

"Her name is Miss Parikh," Raaz said. "She works here at The Bay Blossom, and she lives in the cottage my father was fond of. I came here to find the deed and—"

"Instead you found her," Leo said, grinning.

"Well, yes," Raaz admitted. "She won the deed to the Wednesbury cottage in a game of piquet."

"Did she now?" Leo said. "Well, I'd like to offer Miss Parikh my congratulations."

"Me, too," Percy agreed.

"If it helps matters, she glanced as many times this direction as you did in hers," Leo said.

"Does that mean you counted to two hundred then? Bravo," Raaz said, pushing back his chair from the table and standing as Leo rolled his eyes. It was best to get this over with now.

CHAPTER 11

"AH, MISS PARIKH," LEO SAID WITH A WIDE GRIN. Raaz had led Camelia over to their table. "I thought you seemed familiar, but I couldn't be sure from where we sat. How lovely to see you again."

Unbelievable. His friends had already met Camelia. *How?* The question must've been plainly written on his face, because Percy explained once Camelia and Raaz were both seated around the table.

"If memory serves, we've met before at one of Countess Blair's infamous card parties," Percy said.

His friends awaited Camelia's reaction, seeming to bait her like a cat might engage a mouse to play. But Raaz did not intervene to protect her. She did not need him to, they both knew. Camelia gambled. And won. Her mask was impenetrable. She could hold her own with the beau monde.

"Yes, I recall it now," Camelia said. "Forgive me, my lord, I did not expect to see you here."

"Let's forgo titles, shall we? Please, call me Leo," his friend said, dismissing Camelia's formality with a languid wave.

"And any friend of Raaz's is a friend of ours," Percy added. "I'm Percy."

"Leo and Percy it is, then," Camelia said with a smile. "It's been some time since I was in Mayfair. I trust that Lady Blair is well?"

"Oh, the same as ever," Leo said. "Evelyn loves spending time at places the ton daren't venture."

"Much like you, Miss Parikh," Percy said with a grin. His dark brown hair was longer on top, and he pushed it back from his face as if to better dazzle Camelia with his green eyes. "You should know your friend's quite the danger at the card table, Raaz."

"So I've learned," Raaz muttered, and was satisfied when his words brought a blush to Camelia's face. He hoped she was remembering their card game with as much detail as he was right now.

"Did His Grace tell you about the badger?" Camelia asked Leo.

Raaz scrubbed a hand down his face. Wasn't there anything else to talk about in the Bay besides the dratted badger?

"Oh yes, we heard all about the mighty Basil," Leo said with a chuckle.

"In my mind, it was an evenly matched row," Percy said. "Why, Raaz himself is also reclusive and cantankerous."

Camelia laughed with his friends. Raaz rolled his eyes, but was unable to hold back a chuckle for long.

"So how else have you two been passing your time together in the Bay?" Leo asked.

Perspiration beaded along the back of Raaz's neck. He scrambled for any answer that might stop the vision of his kiss with Camelia, but images from last night slammed into his brain with such force that they rendered him temporarily speechless.

Thankfully, Camelia had more sense, and indeed, more words, and began conversing with his friends about the approaching summer festival. Raaz tried to focus on what she was saying, but only caught snatches of conversation as his mind drifted to their late-night game of vingt-et-un. Again.

Basil, he heard Camelia say, and somehow the badger was even central to the Bay's festival. But no, that wasn't right. As he listened further, she was, in fact, talking about the herb. It was part of a special themed recipe Camelia and Binita were creating for the festival. Then he heard *Ras*—and froze—but she was only mid-word. *Raspberry*, as it turned out, was what she was saying. Because she was still explaining the recipe, of course. Curse his infernal mind. Every word she said called to him, filling him with fever. Every time her pretty, plush lips formed that satisfied *ah*, or her tongue teased a rolling *r*, each sound struck his core, as if she were whispering his name to him under the sheets.

But that was precisely why Camelia wouldn't address Raaz by his given name here at the inn—with other peers, his friends. She kept referring to him with proper titles, and though it bothered him to have such a barrier between them again, he understood the reason for her caution. It would suggest far too much intimacy, and that was exactly the truth of what had bloomed between them last night. It was easier to keep some walls between them, when theirs was a temporary arrangement and they already shared a chamber. A bed. A kiss. A touch.

And still, Raaz wanted more.

"The duke danced," Percy said, scattering Raaz's thoughts. "Here, at the inn?"

"Impossible," Leo added. His ginger-gold hair glinted in the fading light coming through the windows. "Wednesday never even attended balls in London, let alone danced with a single debutante, not when he was—"

Raaz sent his friends a speaking glance and aimed a kick at Leo's shin under the table.

"Not when he was?" Camelia prompted.

"Not when he was better suited to spending an evening at home brooding with his scotch," Percy said in a cheerful manner. "Look at the man, Miss Parikh. Have you ever seen him smile?"

"I'm sure he doesn't know how," Leo agreed.

"That's not true," Camelia said with a quirk of her lips. "I'm looking at his face right now, and he's smiling."

And it was true. He was smiling. How could he not?

Because Raaz was looking at Camelia, too.

BINITA MADE SURE THEY HAD EATEN AT THE BAY Blossom before everyone parted for the evening. Camelia and Raaz said their farewells to Leo and Percy, and then they made their way to the cottage together. The walk was silent, save for the occasional interruption from an insect's hum or birdcall. Wind rustled the leaves in the trees, and waves crashed against the cliffs in the distance. It was a beautiful evening serenade, but Camelia was too lost in her own thoughts to really appreciate the harmony of nature surrounding them, and she suspected the same was true for Raaz.

Seeing Leo and Percy had reminded Camelia, yet again, of how different she and the duke were. She was glad Raaz had the chance to enjoy the company of his friends while in the Bay, but it did not comfort Camelia to learn that she and Raaz had acquaintances in common. She wanted to leave London behind. Raaz had friends who clearly wanted him back there. The fact that she might have passed him before, perhaps even at one of Lady Blair's gatherings, only served to emphasize the insurmountable distance between them. She was a fallen woman who had made mistakes. He was the Duke of Wednesbury. He was not for her—Raaz was out of her reach.

She darted a quick glance in the duke's direction, and even at this moment, he walked too far away to touch. He was solemn and pensive. As severe as a storm brewing, and as beguiling, too. She could all but sense the thoughts and emotions rolling off him with each step.

Or maybe those were simply her feelings.

Despite the terms of their agreement that she'd been the one to set, the arrival of Raaz's friends had disrupted her sense of composure and logic. Now Camelia felt the ticking reminder that their time together was coming to an end. The bursting of the blissful bubble they'd existed in for a few lovely weeks. The end to the elation of hiding from the chaos of the crowded city. The breaking of a storm.

She raised one hand to her cheek to brush away the tears before the duke could notice. But then more droplets fell in rapid succession, and Camelia turned her face up to the sky.

"Rain," Raaz said. And then that distance between them was gone as he tucked her into his side, shielding her with his greatcoat against a sudden gust of air. His warm breath caressed the shell of her ear. "We'll have to make a run for it."

The storm rose around them as they ran the rest of the way up the hill. "Secure the horses and goat in the stable," Camelia shouted as they approached the cottage. "I'll find the cat and bring the clothes in from the line."

CHAPTER 12

RAAZ MANAGED TO COERCE CAMELIA'S MOUNT AND his own black gelding into the stable easily enough before the skies darkened further. But no matter how much Raaz tried to shield the animal from the storm and cajole it to move, the goat would not budge.

"You bedeviling bastard," Raaz cursed. He sprinted to the cottage in the heavy rain. Before opening the door, he ran a hand through his dripping hair, and he tried to avoid tracking too much water inside as he entered.

"What is it?" Camelia asked, and at least Raaz did not have to worry about her being stuck outside in this deluge. He tried to ignore the way her skirts clung to her as Billi wound himself around her legs. "Are you all right?"

"Yes, yes, I'm fine. It's that blasted goat. Never met a more silly, inept, stubborn creature," Raaz said, as he dashed around in a frantic search for an apple to help tempt the goat. After finding the fruit, he ran back to where Bakri was still waiting, entirely unbothered by the commotion.

"You're supposed to have a better sense for bad weather,"

Raaz grumbled, as he offered Bakri the apple in his outstretched palm, coat whipping around him.

The goat simply blinked up at him.

"No," Raaz said in a stern voice. "Don't look at me like that. I won't slice it for you. There's no time."

The goat finally conceded and followed Raaz to safety from the steady torrent of rain.

"Damn you," Raaz said with a sigh, once they were both sheltered in the stable, away from the side where the roof repairs had yet to be finished. "You've made us both a muddy mess."

There was a bit of toweling, thankfully still dry, hanging on a hook, so Raaz cleaned and dried Bakri.

The goat sat down beside Raaz and met his gaze expectantly.

"Fine," Raaz grunted. "I suppose I can wait out the worst of the weather here." He fished in his pocket for his penknife and sliced the apple, feeding it one piece at a time to the satisfied goat who had finally won his way.

Once Bakri was done eating, Raaz peered outside the stable. The rain had slowed to a fine, even mist, and he took advantage of the reprieve to head back into the cottage and see if Camelia needed any help with the washing.

"Oh, no." Camelia took one look at the sodden, grimy state of him and seemed barely able to suppress her laughter. "That's not necessary. Thank you for offering, but I can sort the clothes that need to be cleaned again and the ones decent enough to continue drying. While I hang them on chairs by the fire, why don't you go clean up before the entire cottage smells like a stable, too?"

"I'll heat the water in the hearth upstairs," Raaz said with a nod, because he had neither the pride nor strength left to argue with such a rationale. He left his muddy Hessians and wet stockings near the door, then dragged himself up the steps and into Camelia's room to begin preparing a bath.

After lighting a few candles, boiling the water, and filling the large copper tub, Raaz didn't bother with arranging the screen to keep out any evening drafts. Instead, he let the fire continue to crackle in the hearth, enjoying the way its soothing sound blended with the light rain clinking against the windows and roof. He tore off his wet trousers, braces, shirt, and smalls, and he draped them over the screen's side that was nearest to the hearth. Finally, he set his Pears bar of soap and a sponge on a small stool near the tub and sank into the water with a groan. Raaz leaned his head back against the edge of the bathtub, and he closed his eyes from the sheer pleasure of the warmth.

Although his muscles started to relax as he washed with the soap and sponge, the tension in Raaz's mind did not ease. His thoughts were still on the conversation with his friends at the inn and his plans for additions to the cottage. To begin with, he wanted to build a glasshouse and then perhaps expand the garden. The more he turned the ideas over in his mind, the more he considered the possibility of staying in Robin Hood's Bay. He enjoyed the closeness of the Bay's community and the peace of being in a place that his father had cared for as well. If the Duke of Wednesbury resided here, then it would drive business to the Bay and more visitors—not only for the festival and summers in the country, but at other times of the year, too—especially those with deeper pockets from the ton. Leo and Percy were proof of that already. It would be Raaz's way of honoring his father in a place that had meant a great deal to his parents.

The longer he spent in the country, the less attractive the idea of returning to London became. Raaz enjoyed the freedom from social constraints here. He had privacy that would not be afforded to him as a new, still-unmarried duke in

London where matchmaking mammas would thrust their daughters at him. Most of all, he had the space and time here to think of his father, to turn that grief over inside himself until he might wear its ragged edges smoother. That would allow him to decide what kind of duke, man, and son he wanted to be to keep his father's legacy—and the Wednesbury title—strong.

A spike of guilt rushed in to remind him that his mother and siblings were grieving, too, and he had a responsibility to them as both the eldest son and brother. Well, no matter. If Raaz decided to stay here, then he would bring his family with him to reconnect to the place that was so special to his father, and they, too, could revel in the peace and pace of life in the country. For now, his younger brother Rohan had all but demanded that Raaz let him manage things while Raaz went to Robin Hood's Bay.

The only question was how to convince Camelia that, if he did remain longer in the village, it wasn't because he expected more from her. She'd been clear about the terms of their arrangement, and he'd agreed. One week, or as long as it took to finish the remaining work on the cottage. And he would never go back on his word.

But if, after some time, she found herself wanting more time together, too, then he would be happy to revisit their terms. Raaz could wait for the change to the agreement to come from Camelia, but he would not expect anything more from her than she was willing to give. In the meantime, there were plenty of other projects he was passionate about pursuing here.

Entertaining visions of his perfect future in the Bay only made Raaz's mind eager to ply him with other wishful fantasies. He knew better, he truly did. And yet, he also knew Camelia was downstairs. Right at this very minute, she could be shedding the wet clothing from her skin as he had done only moments before. *You dunderhead, she isn't going to waltz around the cottage in the nude.*

But if that thought was intended to dissuade his mind from its current trajectory, it in fact did the exact opposite. Raaz gave in as all the blood in his body started to slink southward to his groin. Now, all he could see was golden sunlight streaming in like honey and illuminating her mouthwatering bare bronze skin. *It's night, and it's raining right now. You can hear it. You absolute scapegrace.* Raaz ignored the badgering of his better judgment. Who cared? He was alone.

And his cock was ready. Hard, heavy, and aching. Fuck, he was always primed when it came to her. He had promised himself he wouldn't spend until he had at least been inside Camelia once. But his mind hadn't communicated that message with the rest of him. His body still wanted her. *Needed* her. And since she wasn't here, able, and enthusiastic —his hand was going to have to do the job.

Something about spending time with Leo and Percy had made her pensive. If that, combined with the chaos of the storm, made Camelia too tired or otherwise uninterested in seeking pleasure with him tonight, he would accept that without question. But if she did desire intimacy, it still wouldn't hurt to tame the beast of his desire so that he did not overwhelm her tonight. He did not want to alarm her with the intensity of his ardor. They should take things at a pace that would ensure her comfort and pleasure. Even if they did nothing more than simply sleep next to each other again, he would be happy. Raaz desired her trust above all, and he never wanted to make her uncomfortable. He'd sooner die than have that.

It was fine. He'd closed the door. And he would be quick about it. God, he'd been half-hard all day from craving Camelia, so it should be easy enough. But he would have to be quiet. And that might prove most difficult.

Still, Raaz was resolved to try his damnedest. He skimmed his palm down his body, dipped under the surface of the water, and wrapped his rough hand around his shaft. His skin burned hotter than the temperature of the tub. In all the places where she had touched him through his clothes when they kissed. And especially in all the places he hadn't yet felt her body. Or her hands. Or her mouth.

Everything around him was warm, slick, and wet. It took very little of his ambitious creativity to supply the rest, especially when fueled by the sensation and sound of splashing water. Still, it was a struggle to organize the images flashing in the darkness behind his eyelids before they disappeared. He tugged his cock in a few long, slow, sliding strokes from the base to the head and back down, then added a twisting motion with a firmer grip.

Raaz thought first of that beautiful hair. Every time he saw Camelia's plait, he wanted to wrap it around his fist and pull her face to his. All that endless inky silk. He harbored a tendre for that thick curtain of tresses. Raaz wanted it in his face, then brushing his chest as she moved lower, the cool touch of the strands caressing his skin. Then she'd pull it all to one side, or toss it behind her shoulders, or secure it with a ribbon, just before she bent to— *Fuck.*

Her tongue, and that same sweet mouth he'd tasted, would taste him as she licked every inch. Raaz worked himself with more pressure as he brought to mind her soft raspberry lips and saw them closing around his cock, taking him in deep. God, how he wanted her grazing his collarbone with her teeth, nipping at his neck. He'd do the same to the delicate skin at the hollow of her throat and bite the place where her pulse beat. Mark her, if she'd let him. Hell, she could mark him, too, if she wanted.

Raaz wanted to lace his fingers with hers and never let go as they made slow, languorous love. And damn, but how good she'd feel, touching him the way he was touching himself now. Better, even, he was sure. He wanted to selfishly enjoy her cupping his balls and massaging them, stroking him until he was a writhing creature in her hands. A mess of a man she could command. He'd teach Camelia how to please him—that he enjoyed a little teasing torment. He liked it fast and rough. Or soft and slow. He didn't mind being made to wait and could handle whatever she wanted to give him. Or not—he enjoyed being denied too. Within limits, of course—it made release all the more intense.

Sweet merciful heaven above, and her tits. Fuck, he'd not even touched them last night, and he had no one other than himself to blame for not going further. But Raaz had had his reasons. And they were good ones. Even if it didn't seem that way now. He hadn't wanted to combust on the spot. If he'd taken the time to tease and bite and suck those pretty nipples he'd seen pebbled through her damp bodice today—to worship each breast with his tongue and mouth as she deserved—then he'd have had nothing left to give her later. But now he could indulge in how perfect it would feel to get his cock between those lovely breasts. How much he wanted to fuck those gorgeous tits until he came all over her soft, sweet skin. Because this was a dream. None of it was real. And every carnal urge could stay hidden.

He groaned. The guttural sound echoed in the chamber, too loud and obscene even to his own ears, but he couldn't stop himself. To see her painted like that was too much for Raaz. His breathing was labored and uneven as he fucked his own fist, stroking harder and faster, twitching against his palm. God, he hadn't even touched Camelia between her thighs yet. How he wanted nothing more than to coat his fingers in her silky arousal before licking each one clean and feasting on her quim. If she desired it, he'd let her ride his face as many times as she wanted before he even slid his cock inside her cunt. He'd make her feel as good as he felt right now, and so much more. Raaz wanted to taste her on his tongue for days after. He squeezed his shaft, applying more pressure near the head, and wished it was her hand instead of his.

"Fuck," he moaned. He was so close. "Yes, Camelia. That's it, sweetheart."

Suddenly, there was a sharp intake of breath behind him, followed by a surprised yelp and scrambling footsteps. And then the sound of the door snicking shut.

What in the bloody hell was going on? Raaz whipped around to try and understand. He stared at the door to the room, which was closed.

No. Impossible. He couldn't have missed something as stupid as making sure the door was shut all the way. Could he have? Hadn't he checked twice? Raaz was sure he had. He was . . . he was a damned numbskull, that's what. This was what he deserved for thinking with his prick instead of his brain.

He hadn't even had the chance to envision what bliss it would be to bury himself to the hilt inside Camelia's soft, wet quim. And now there was no time. He stepped out of the tub and threw on his banyan, hoping he could salvage whatever damage had been done.

A knock sounded behind him, and he froze. "Yes?" he replied.

He heard the door open and his name in her voice. "Raaz?"

She said it in the same exact breathy way he'd imagined the entire time he'd had his cock in hand. But he didn't dare turn around. Let her express her shock freely, and then they could both avoid looking at each other as they left the room and regained their composure. They never had to speak of it again.

He cleared his throat. "How much of that did you see?" he asked. "How much of that did you hear?"

A few long moments of silence followed his questions, and

Raaz winced. *Fucking idiot.* He shouldn't have called out her name. He shouldn't have been so loud. Above all, he shouldn't have *forgotten to close the door*. It had been a reckless mistake. The kind a green lad might make, not a man at his age.

"I didn't see anything," Camelia said at last, and her throaty rasp heated his blood again. "I heard my name. I heard you call me sweetheart. But it was not nearly enough."

Of all the things he had expected her to say, this was the furthest from any of them. She was most assuredly going to be the death of him. And yet, Raaz said, "Well, if you're going to watch, then you should come inside. The view's better from here."

Because he was still thinking with his shameless prick.

CHAPTER 13

CAMELIA STEPPED INSIDE, WALKED UP BEHIND HIM, and waited. He still did not turn around, so she slid her palms along his back over the embroidered dark blue silk of the Indian dressing gown he wore. She mapped each muscle that rippled across his broad shoulders and then dragged her hands lower until she reached the base of his spine. When he shivered, it sent a thrill racing through her. It was *her* touch that made this intimidating, imposing, mountain of a man crumble. And she smiled at that.

Raaz slowly turned to meet her gaze and caught both of her hands in his large, warm palms.

"I—" Camelia blinked. It was as though she had been bewitched moments before. "Oh, no. Forgive me, I don't know what— That was terribly inappropriate. I'm so sorry."

"Whatever for?" Raaz said, releasing her hands from his grasp. "You can touch me any time you want. Any way you want."

Unfortunately for her, he'd tied the belt of his banyan, but Camelia still allowed her eyes to travel down his body and then back up to his face.

Raaz arched a single brow, and she saw the obvious amusement on his face in the smirk he tried to hide. But if he thought her gaze was too brazen, then he did not say it, and she was glad. Camelia's gaze darted to the tub. "Did you f—"

"Oh, that," Raaz interjected with a weak laugh, gesturing at the door. "Ah, *yes*. I am sorry for that."

He ran a hand through his wet, dark hair. It was longer now than the first day he had arrived at the cottage, and the locks had started to curl with dampness. Camelia's fingers itched to touch his hair, too.

"You apologize for—" She hesitated. "Finishing?"

"What? No," Raaz said in a rush. "Why would you— *No*."

"So then, you don't apologize?" Camelia asked with a tilt of her head.

It wasn't right to tease him—this man with too much on his mind already. Yet, she could not resist. Camelia wanted to make him smile, or even better, laugh. She wanted to see the austere angles of his face soften, because she had watched it happen before. With his friends and with the people of the Bay. He was always beautiful, of course, but especially when he was unguarded.

Raaz closed his eyes, scrubbed a hand down his face, and muttered an oath under his breath.

Camelia waited and fought not to laugh.

When he opened his eyes, Raaz said, "Evidently, I *forgot* to check the door was properly shut, and I apologize for not telling you I was going to use the hearth in your room. The chamber my luggage is currently in has a coal fireplace. We should replace the thatched roof on the cottage next or make sure all the rooms have space to burn wood only." He sighed. "And, no, I didn't finish. Does that help?"

"Yes," she said with a small nod. "Thank you. I'm sorry for approaching the door and watching, as it were. But I heard

90

you"—she paused—"making noises, and from down the hall, I thought you might be in pain."

"In pain?" Raaz said the two words very slowly, and she saw the laughter shining in his dark eyes.

"Yes. You could have hurt yourself out there in the storm trying to get all the animals into the stable and only realized once you were in the bath." Camelia gave a vague wave of her hand, and a giggle escaped her. "Or you might have fallen into or out of the tub."

"And that's something to delight over, I see," Raaz said dryly. "How comforting."

"No, no, of course not," Camelia said through gasping breaths. But her protest would have been more convincing if she wasn't currently dissolving into a fit of mirth. "I worried, too, that you were visited by a badger friend of Basil's, and that's when I had to come find you before my imagination got the best of me."

"Again with the plaguing badgers," Raaz grumbled. "Will we never be rid of them?"

Camelia laughed freely now, and so did he. It was a rich, deep, warm sound. She wanted to lay her head against his chest and feel the rumble of his laughter in time with the beating of his heart. But she did not move closer. Yet.

When Raaz's laughter had subsided, he cocked his head and studied her. His eyes drifted down her body and snagged on her bare legs. "Is that my shirt you're wearing?" His question was a hoarse scrape of sound.

"Ah, I'm sorry," Camelia said, heat rising to her cheeks. "All our other clothes were still wet from the rain." It was too bold of her, she knew, and yet she liked the way the fine, soft lawn felt against her skin, how it allowed her to be close to him without being *too* close or frightening Raaz away.

A muscle jumped in Raaz's jaw. "There's still more water heating on the hearth. You can use it, if you want, and tell me what else your imagination suggested I might be doing in the bath."

He wasn't laughing now, and neither was she.

To be sure, Camelia wanted more. But that meant she would have to let Raaz see more of her, too. She'd have to leave behind the hurts of her past that had followed her from India to London and from London to the Bay. And that was what frightened her the most—how much she already wanted to trust him and forget everything else from before.

"I can bring a second tub, if that would make you more comfortable—though that one's a hip bath, so it won't be large enough for the both of us," he said. "Or I can leave you alone, if that will put you more at ease," he added in haste, perhaps misunderstanding the reason for her quiet indecision. "Yes. Obviously. I should have started by saying that. How wildly arrogant to presume otherwise. Of course you'd want privacy." He turned away as he continued rambling.

Camelia reached out and laced her fingers with his. "No. Stay. Please."

The duke remained where he stood, and Camelia kept her hand locked in his. She walked to the copper tub, and he helped her step into the water. In another world, on another night, he might have been extending his arm to assist her out of a coach, escort her into supper, or spin her across a parquet floor. But this was even better. Because this was just the two of them. Alone. Together. For now, at least, and she would make her peace with that.

Camelia stood in the water, facing him, waiting for what happened next.

"You're sure?" he asked.

She nodded.

"Camelia, I need the words." He gave a dark laugh. "I need to know I'm not still in one of my feral, lust-driven fevers."

"Yes," she said. "I'm certain." Every inch of her was on fire, so if he was struck by a fever, then so, too, was she. The duke had invited her in, and now, well, she didn't know exactly what all this meant, but she wasn't going to stop or leave before she found out.

"You look lovely in my shirt," he said, fingering the edge of the soaked hem. "Now, take it off."

He helped her pull it over her head and then tossed it onto the chair next to the tub.

Raaz's eyes were hot and dark. They reflected the candle-light back at her from their blazing depths. Camelia had never had a man study her with such intensity before.

He was still covered. She was not.

And so, she took as much of that heated focus as she could handle.

Before she remembered that she had been burned before.

Camelia folded her arms over herself, dipping her head and breaking his gaze.

"No, don't," Raaz said, voice rough and low. He stepped closer to her. "Please. Never hide yourself from me, Camelia. You're so lovely. Beautiful beyond words."

She was without words, too. Camelia did not meet his eyes but curled her fingers into his banyan to pull him nearer. He came to her willingly. She slid her fingers down until she reached the belt, and then she met his gaze.

"You can do whatever you want to me, Camelia," Raaz said again. "God, please just touch me, sweetheart."

She bit her lower lip. "I want to," she said. "But I need you to answer some questions for me first."

"Of course," Raaz agreed. "Anything you need."

"Thank you," Camelia said. She let the silk belt of his banyan slide through her fingers before she stepped to one side of the tub to allow him access into the water.

She was going to do this with the duke tonight—of that, she was sure. But she wanted to be more certain of other things, too, like why Raaz had wanted to stay and manage the repairs to the stable roof himself once he knew the deed was genuinely hers. Even if it did matter to him that the property be maintained, it would have been just as easy for him to send for his man of business.

She was not foolish enough to believe he'd stayed for her, and that was precisely why she wanted to know what kept him here—hiding from London.

Raaz unbelted his banyan, letting it slide from his shoulders until it fell to the floor in a pool of Prussian blue silk. The duke stepped into the tub and gently pulled her down into the water with him. Camelia wished Raaz would have waited so that she could have looked properly and memorized each hard plane and angle, every last long, thick inch of him. But she was too stunned to say the words, and the moment passed.

"Come here," Raaz said in a sinister, velvet-dark tone that did something strange to her insides. "First, we'll talk. Then we'll do whatever you're thinking that has you looking at me like that."

CHAPTER 14

SHE SAT FACING HIM, AND THEIR LEGS TANGLED together as they took each other in. It was silent, save for the rain still plinking on the roof and against the glass windowpanes. The candlelight and flames from the hearth danced across the walls, occasionally casting her and Raaz in a fiery glow before they were bathed in shadows again. It was a heavy silence, full of unspoken promises. The kind of alert, tense quiet that meant they were both waiting for someone to do something.

A bar of soap sat on the stool beside the tub. Camelia picked it up and handed it to Raaz before turning around and sliding backward to sit nestled between his legs. She pulled her plaited hair over one shoulder so her back was exposed to him. "Make yourself useful, Your Grace."

"Minx," he said with a low laugh, and the warm gust of breath tickled the nape of her neck. A familiar light fragrance of orange, almond, and bergamot enveloped them as he used the soap, letting it—and his hands—slowly glide across her shoulders and down her back. He gave her time to grow accustomed to his touch. To crave more of it. Almost to ask for more of it.

"It's my soap," he said with a tightness to his words. "Is that all right?"

"Yes, it's fine," she answered, because she was afraid to reveal more. She wouldn't have worn his shirt if she didn't want to smell like his soap, his skin, like *him*.

She turned to see him more clearly. "I never realized you had silver hair here," she said, running her fingers along his temples.

"Have a care for my dignity, woman," Raaz growled. "I didn't invite you in to mock my old age."

She pressed her back against his warm chest and nuzzled his neck. "And precisely how ancient are you, Your Grace?"

"Four and thirty," Raaz said with an amused huff. "Yourself?"

"Nine and twenty," Camelia answered. "Your mumma hasn't wanted you to marry, especially now that you've come into a title?"

"Ah, the first question." Raaz gave a weary laugh. "I am sure my mother would have no objection to the idea."

Camelia was silent, watching his hands lather soap down her arms with gentle care.

"You can ask me, Camelia," Raaz said. "I'll tell you anything you want."

But still, she could not find the courage.

The duke did not rush her, only lathered his hands and placed the bar of soap back on the stool. Then he smoothed soap across her collarbone and in the valley between her breasts. His palms cupped and caressed them, and when he dragged the pads of his thumbs across her nipples, Camelia gasped, arching back against his shoulder and exposing her throat to him.

"Too much?" Raaz whispered against the shell of her ear, before lightly grazing it with his teeth and tugging on the lobe.

She inhaled a sharp breath. "Not enough."

"Good," he said, rolling her nipples between his thumb and forefinger. He pinched and squeezed as he kissed a path from her jaw to the curve of her shoulder. He bit the top of her shoulder, and the sting tore a moan from her throat. He laved the spot with his tongue.

"Raaz," Camelia pleaded. She placed her hands over his as Raaz played with her breasts. He stilled, and she waited for one brief, blissful moment before dragging his touch away. Then she turned and placed a hand on his chest to stop him.

"Yes?" Raaz said, dazed eyes roving from her neck to her breasts.

"You're distracting me," she whispered.

"And that's a bad thing?" he asked. He pulled back, and his eyes were dark pools of desire—pupils blown wide with wanting. The force of the lust there made her own breath catch as he lifted her hand and interlaced their fingers.

"It is," she murmured, though she hated to stop him.

"Why?" he asked, raising her hand to his lips and brushing a kiss across her knuckles.

"Because we're not done talking."

"Yes, that's true." He sighed and released her hand. "You're right, of course. I got carried away."

"So did I." She smiled, but it quickly faded because she couldn't go any further before she knew the truth. "Raaz?"

"Yes, my darling," he said, stretching his arms out to rest on the edge of the tub.

"You never said if there was—*is*—such a person in your life, someone that you wish to marry." She tried not to stumble through the words, because they were necessary, and yet, that did not make it less difficult. If there was a woman in London, or elsewhere, then she had to know. It was not fair to her or this other woman, whoever she may be. She should have asked before they'd kissed last night, but they'd both been too swept up in the moment to talk.

"No, sweetheart," he said, and his warm arms banded around her shoulders. "I would never do this otherwise. There's no one else."

She tipped her face up to him. Raaz hummed with appreciation and kissed her. The instant his lips touched hers, Camelia opened for him, eager to tangle her tongue with his, to taste the truth in his words. The soft, sweet slide of their mouths combined with the firm heat of his arousal behind her was almost too much to bear. She tried to move against him, seeking friction, desperate for relief. But Raaz held her in place.

"Ignore it," he said, and she was pleased to hear his words were labored and heated with lust. "I am."

"I can't," she said. It was a wonder he thought she had more strength than he did.

"Yes, it's hard as hell, I know," he said with a languid laugh against her lips. "Pardon the double entendre, but it's quite difficult to master oneself in the proximity of such irresistible temptation. This is the best I can do. You'll have to forgive me."

"No," she said, pressing closer. "I don't want to forgive you. And I don't want to ignore it."

Raaz swore and cradled her face with both hands. "Then who am I to stop you, love."

Camelia couldn't be sure who lunged at who this time, but it was hotter, hungrier. More insistent and impatient. It was one long, honeyed kiss that never seemed to end. As if they each refused to come up for air before the other and risk breaking the spell. Raaz ran his thumb along the line of her jaw and adjusted their angle to taste her more deeply. Camelia was as urgent and unleashed. But the duke had taken his chance to explore, and she hadn't. Despite all her patience before, now she couldn't resist. She thrust her hand under the surface of the water and found the heat of his erection. She curled her palm around his cock, swiped the pad of her thumb lightly across the head, and gave him one tentative stroke.

"Fuck, Camelia," he said, breaking their kiss. He spoke in that same dark voice as before, when she'd caught him and shut the door. It did wild things to her, hearing her name in that delicious tone, feeling it slip under her skin and into her blood. She wanted to feel his coarse words on her skin, against every part of her.

He covered her hand with his, and he guided her to touch him in the way he wanted. She gripped him harder and moved her hand faster. Raaz was falling apart in front of her with every shallow, harsh breath. She could feel it in her hands, taste it through the searing, open-mouthed kisses they shared as he moaned into her mouth.

When he threw his head back and groaned, the deep sound made a home low in her core, flooding her body with liquid heat. Camelia's skin was tight and feverish, and even lower, her quim pulsed, desperately wanting the thick, hard length of him to be inside her.

He closed his eyes, surrendering to her, completely lost to bliss. But Camelia kept her eyes open. She would not miss a single minute of watching him wanting her and what she was doing to him. He was a vision, and this was her chance to look her fill, without him knowing how much she wanted to keep him like this forever. In her mind. In her heart. In her home. In her life.

Some of his dark hair fell over his brow while the rest of it stuck out at every angle, tousled from her own fingers tangling in it. She liked seeing the evidence of her on him. The whiskers on his face had grown in more fully now, and she loved the wilder, dangerous, more disheveled quality that lent him too.

Tonight, when she was this close to him, Camelia had learned that Raaz's irises were, in fact, almost russet, like cognac. She'd noticed the warmth in his dark brown eyes before, but now she had a name for the exact shade—another detail about him she could keep hidden away in her memories. His brown skin was warmer from the time he spent outside, and she raised one hand to trace the flush along his cheeks and down his throat before following it with her lips and tongue.

Suddenly, his eyes flew open, and he wrapped his fingers around her wrist. "That's enough for now," he said between ragged breaths, and brought the back of her hand to his lips for a kiss.

Camelia was stunned. Surely, it couldn't be enjoyable for him to remain in his current state. It certainly wasn't enjoyable for her to be left so . . . unsatisfied. Had she done something wrong? Was that why he wanted her to stop?

"Are you certain— You don't need to . . ." She let her questions trail off, suddenly feeling too timid even after all they'd done in this tub together, and even after their earlier discussion of him not finishing.

"You're perfect, and don't worry. You can do more than that before you risk unmanning me," Raaz said. His eyes were alight with mischief and challenge. "I promise I'll let you play with me as much as you like. But later, sweetheart. Not now."

"Why?" She didn't like the breathiness in her voice.

"Because we haven't finished talking," he said with a wicked grin, turning her own wise words against her.

He brought her hand to his chest and released it, then leaned his head back, closing his eyes again as she ran her fingers through his hair and down his face and neck. She paused when she found old scars on the skin at the base of his throat and along his collarbone. They must have been hidden by his cravat all this time. She traced them with her fingers— three in total, all on the left side. The one at the base of his throat was longer, and looked as though someone had held a knife there and tried to slice clean across. Then there were two smaller scars, the first along his collarbone and the second above his heart, only just missing it.

"Thankfully, my face was spared," Raaz said in a quiet, wry voice. "Terrible, aren't they?"

"No," she said, sliding her hand until it rested on his heart. "Not at all."

She'd had no idea he'd been watching her, and she didn't want to offend him by continuing to stare in fascination. But it was the truth. They were not terrible. She couldn't very well tell him that his scars were *lovely*. He'd think her disingenuous, that she was only saying it to coddle his pride. Raaz wouldn't believe the words, or worse, would be hurt by them, and she'd never want that. Besides, it didn't even come close to capturing what she meant.

In truth, she didn't need the *-ly* at the end of the word at all.

She'd made Raaz agree to only one week of pleasure and told him there would be nothing more between them than that. She'd promised herself she would not fall in love too fast again.

And yet, love was not limited by time.

There were, however, other confines to consider. The ones that meant a duke could not marry a ruined woman. So, she could not tell him that she loved his scars. But he was here with her now, and that was enough. Camelia was so thankful he was alive, and that a deck of cards and a deed had brought the duke to her door. *Mine*, her brain insisted. But that was the most dangerous word of all. Because he would never be hers to have.

"Say it again," Raaz whispered.

"What?" she asked, and it was only then that Camelia realized she'd spoken the word aloud. She turned her head away and curled her fingers around the edge of the tub to avoid touching him again. Nothing good would come of that. It only led her to blurt out thoughts that were best kept to herself.

"Camelia." Raaz said her name with such tender intimacy. The sound was sweeter than any other endearments he'd showered her with tonight. He tipped her chin toward him. "Don't make me ask again. Please."

She couldn't look at him, not when he was looking at her like that. Those cognac eyes were softer than she'd ever seen. But she couldn't look away from him, either. Camelia was helpless to refuse the duke anything, nor did she want to, so she did the only thing she could.

"Mine," she said, and this time, tears filled her eyes. She did not want Raaz to see her cry, so she ducked her head to kiss his lowest scar first before moving up to the next one, then the last, then his jaw, his cheek, his lips. Camelia smiled when she felt tears on his face, too. How fortunate she was that they were both fools. She covered his face in kisses, licking the salt from his skin until he was laughing, and so was she.

CHAPTER 15

RAAZ WAS THE WORST OF LIARS. BY SOME MIRACLE, Camelia believed what he'd said, but he didn't at all have the same self-mastery with her that he did alone. When she kissed his scars, he was seconds away from spilling against her thigh. Only his fervent desire not to take his own pleasure before he'd given it to her—ideally, more than once—kept him from coming undone. Besides, she still had more questions, and giving her the answers would make everything better. For both of them. He wanted to put her mind at ease to help her enjoy their physical pleasure even more.

After rinsing the soap clean from Camelia and himself, they dried themselves off. Raaz wrapped Camelia in one of his freshly laundered dressing gowns and found a clean banyan for himself. He added more wood to the fire. They sat on one of the sofas together, listening to the crackling flames and watching the rain dance along the windows.

Camelia squeezed the water from her hair with a length of toweling and then went to her bedside table. She returned to the sofa with a hairbrush.

"Please," Raaz said, holding out his hand. "Allow me."

"Oh, that's not—" Camelia said, ducking her head with a demure blush. "I can manage myself."

"I know," he said. "But that's not why I asked. I love your hair, and I want to do it. So, let me. Please."

Her sudden shyness was both absurd and endearing. They'd just been naked together, and he intended to be naked with her again very soon. All night, in fact, if she desired that, too. For fuck's sake, she'd expertly held his cock in her hand only minutes before, and this was what made her blush? Something in his chest squeezed so tight he thought it might break, and Raaz was unable to resist grinning.

"If you insist," she said with a small smile, and gave Raaz the brush.

"Thank you," he murmured, and turned her so that she faced the cheval glass in the corner of the room. "I do."

Raaz brushed out Camelia's long hair with gentle strokes to avoid tangling the wet tresses. When he was done, she passed him a small glass vial of oil. He tipped a few drops into his palm and warmed it up between his hands. A burst of that same heavenly lemon and lavender combination he'd been searching for since the first day he met her greeted him, and he paused as that subtle third scent tantalized him again. He brought his hands to his nose and breathed in. *Jasmine.* He almost groaned with the satisfaction of having finally recognized it.

He worked the oil into her hair, gently massaging her scalp. Camelia let out a soft moan, and the sound shot straight to his groin. His blood heated. She was so damned responsive to him, and he loved that. Raaz could get used to this—to her —too quickly, perhaps. *But she only wants you for one week.* He frowned.

He realized he'd been lost in thought when she reached behind her head and wrapped her fingers around his wrists.

She guided him to work the oil down toward the middle and ends of her hair.

It was the hint of jasmine that would torment him the most, he knew. Already, it taunted him with visions of Camelia wearing a gajra of white jasmine flowers wrapped around her plait. Her ankles, adorned with delicate payal, would peek out from beneath the hem of a heavily beaded and embroidered ruby red lehnga. And later that night, when it was just the two of them again, he would take down her hair, undress her with great care, and remove everything except the anklets he had given her as a gift for their wedding day. He would kiss her palms and trace the mehndi designs with his tongue until he found his name hidden in the red henna on her skin.

Raaz curled his hands into fists to stop himself from reaching for Camelia. It was too much. He was damned near trembling from all the pain of wanting, and somehow, inexplicably, also on the verge of tears. Camelia Parikh and Raaz Panchal. Camelia Panchal, his mind suggested, was the only reasonable answer. The natural next step. As if it were the correct solution to some equation Raaz hadn't realized he was trying to solve.

He had to get a hold of himself. Because she didn't want that. Or at least, she didn't think it could happen. Surely to her, a marriage between them was impossible. But Raaz had thought finding someone like Camelia had been impossible, and yet, here she was, right in front of his eyes. In the cottage his father loved. Close enough to touch. To keep. Like she had been made for him from the start.

And he didn't roll his eyes at the thoughts he was having. Because he realized that these sentiments were serious.

True, he'd so far avoided being paired up, in no small part because he'd evaded every possible trap for marriage that he could. And yes, he'd been okay with that. For a while.

Until now. Until her.

But now, he recalled tales about how his parents had met, and the letters they had read aloud about relatives and friends in India finding love and marrying, too. Raaz and his younger brother hadn't paid as much attention as their three younger sisters, perhaps, but they'd listened nevertheless, and somewhere in Raaz's heart, these stories—from a place he'd never seen, but learned all the same—made a home. These Indian threads wove together with his life in England, creating a tapestry of experience that was both new and familiar. New, in the sense that Raaz had not known how much he longed to meet someone he could share languages and a culture with. Familiar, in the sense that he was looking at her right now and recognizing that these dreams had possibly been there all along, but not shown themselves to him until he met Camelia. He was surprising himself. He was changing, or maybe simply becoming more himself. These hopes inside him had been there the entire time, or she drew them forth. Whatever the reason for his feelings, it was all sudden and startling, and yet somehow exactly as it should be. This was what he'd been waiting for. *She* was who he'd been waiting for. It was right for him to want to marry her and make her his duchess.

Except for one problem. He still had to convince Camelia. He would have to take what was left of their time working on the stable roof and show her. He was the damned Duke of Wednesbury, and while she must see his title as an obstacle, he saw it as an opportunity to prove to her there was nothing that would stand in his way. Not even her own doubts. He would never dismiss them, of course, but he could help dismantle them. Whatever she might be afraid of, he would show her that she had nothing to fear from him. And together, they could make this work.

"Raaz?" Camelia asked, meeting his gaze in the mirror. "Are you all right?"

"Ah, yes," he lied. "Do you have a ribbon?"

"Yes," she said. She reached behind them to hand him a length of velvet, and he set it on the low table near them.

"I can do three sections or four," Raaz said. "Any more than that, and I'm afraid it gets a bit hopeless."

"Three is fine, thank you," Camelia said with a soft laugh. "It's how I typically wear my hair."

"So I've noticed," Raaz said, and he wasn't sure what possessed him to admit such a ridiculous thing. He'd already said he loved her hair. And that should have been enough—because she'd made it clear she did not want more from him. So there was no earthly reason why he'd had to reveal he paid attention to how she styled her hair each day. Let alone that he knew it was in a three-strand plait most of the time. But his damned mind and mouth were hell-bent on scheming together to make sure he appeared a besotted bewakoof.

"Oh," Camelia said. Pink painted her cheeks, and Raaz supposed that, at least, made his foolish confession worth it. "A little less tension, please, would be fine for the nighttime. Better not to risk a headache."

"As you wish," Raaz said.

They were both quiet as he divided her hair into three equal sections and plaited them together, taking his time to make sure no tendrils escaped or were left out and that the tension was slack, yet even.

His hands grazed her back as he wove her hair. Camelia was warm and soft, and smelled so damned sweet. Raaz swallowed, salivating like a fucking animal that wanted to devour her—and, well, that was the truth. Indeed, he did want to sink his teeth into the tempting curve of her heart-shaped bottom and taste her everywhere that she would let him until she trembled against his tongue.

"How are you so skilled at this?" she asked, interrupting his libidinous longings.

For a moment he wondered if she was asking how he was so accomplished at managing to outwardly function at the most minimal level while simultaneously maintaining a spectacularly salacious mind. When a spire of sense finally emerged from his mental fog of filth, Raaz realized Camelia was asking about his prowess with plaiting hair.

"I've had a lot of practice," he said, and the assertion also applied to his predilection for prurience.

"Really?" Camelia tried to face him, but he tugged her hair, and she turned back to the mirror.

"Mmm, yes. Required curriculum at Cambridge, my dear," he drawled.

"Oh, do be serious, Your Grace," she reprimanded him with a laugh. "Please."

It was this final word, so small and so softly uttered, that did it. Camelia's plea struck Raaz's heart with all the delicate strength of a rose petal. And yet, it succeeded in slicing his sardonic shield to shreds. How much more could he take before he was wholly unraveled? Fuck, she'd seen his tears, and then he'd almost cried *again* imagining her as his bride. *His wife.*

Raaz exhaled a heavy breath. Tears were something he hadn't even witnessed in himself, let alone shared with anyone else, for years. It would seem they still had much further to go to plumb the depths of their past together tonight.

CHAPTER 16

"I HAVE THREE YOUNGER SISTERS. MY YOUNGER brother and I would often help my mother plait their hair. Sometimes my father would help, too, if they complained there was a bump that wouldn't lay flat, or an uneven section." Raaz laughed and then tied her velvet ribbon in a bow around the end of the plait. "We could at least manage the simpler styles." He caught her under the chin with two fingers, and tilted her head to the side so she could see her hair, hoping his efforts would meet with her approval.

"You miss them," Camelia said, as she inspected his handiwork in the cheval glass. Apparently satisfied, she pulled her braid over one shoulder.

"Yes," Raaz said, though she hadn't said the words like a question. He ran his fingers through his hair to avoid wasting any remaining oil. Then he stood and went to the dressing table to wash. He poured water from the ewer into the small basin there.

"My next question," Camelia said. "Why did you stay here in the Bay, instead of returning to be with them in London?"

Ah. He wiped his hands with the toweling and stared out the window into the darkness.

"That has to do with my father. It's difficult to know where to begin." He swallowed. "He was a scholar at heart. Always a much gentler soul than I, or my mother and siblings. Now that I'm older, I see more of him in me, and I'm glad I haven't lost him, not entirely." He turned to face Camelia.

"Oh, Raaz, I'm so sorry," Camelia said, coming to him and wrapping her arms around his waist. "Please, forgive me. We needn't discuss anything you don't want to, but I am happy you have that reminder of him every day in yourself."

"Thank you. Yes, I am, too. But we didn't always see eye to eye, especially when I was younger." Raaz laughed and pulled her against his side, leading them back to the sofa. When he was half-sitting, with the soft curves of her body nestled against him—distractingly so—he continued. "Well, I say *we*, but the truth is *I* was the stubborn one. I had little regard for anyone else's rules or order and didn't hesitate to get into scrapes."

His banyan had fallen open to reveal his torso, and Camelia traced a finger over his chest. He knew she was too compassionate to ask about his scars outright.

Raaz pulled up the sleeve of his banyan to show her the inside of his forearm. "There's a faint scar here from a foolish bout of foxed fencing with my brother, Rohan. To be quite honest, we were both lucky that neither of us lost a limb that day." He laughed. "But the other three are from reckless times with Leo and Percy, and helping Aarav break up a brawl at The Tiger after a lord too deep into his cups wouldn't accept his loss at the tables."

"Thank you for sharing that with me," she said. After a moment's pause, she asked, "Why were you fencing with your brother while in your cups?"

The question surprised him, and he chuckled. "*That's* the

scar you want to ask about? Not the one that nearly sliced my throat or stabbed through my heart?"

"I certainly won't mind if you wish to tell me about the others," Camelia said. She placed a hand on his forearm. "But I supposed the situation with your brother would be the most benign to talk about since it seemed like the least threatening injury. If the location of the scar isn't anything to judge by, then please correct me."

"That's very kind." He pressed a kiss to her forehead. "It was ages ago at this point, but Rohan, Leo, Percy, and I were trapped for twenty days at a dreadfully boring house party. We decided to forgo playing pall-mall as scheduled in favor of imbibing and fencing along the garden paths for wagers instead—without any of the appropriate attire, mind you."

He felt her smile against his chest. "Truly?" she said. "I can't imagine you doing such a thing. Leo and Percy? Yes, that makes sense. But you?"

"In fact, it was my idea," he said with a grin, and she laughed. The sound vibrated through him, and it reminded him that he wasn't mired in the past any longer. "I know. It's difficult to believe when you look at me now. But we entertained the young ladies well enough, and I'll admit that was a large part of the daftness. I believe some women even started a betting pool on our routs and victories."

Camelia gave him a playful swat on his forearm. He grinned and rubbed his scar in mock outrage.

"Not to worry. No one else was injured beyond a few bruises. Only me. But I suppose it's no less than I deserved for starting the whole mad affair." He laughed. "And rest assured, we were promptly sent packing that very same day, but I think that alone made it worth it."

"Oh, Raaz, stop," she rebuked him, but it would have been more convincing if she wasn't failing to stifle her giggles.

"There must have been an easier way to escape than risking bodily harm."

"I'm sure there was," he agreed. "But our idea was the fastest, and I don't think you understand how desperate we were to get away from that miserable excuse for a party. My dear brother was fending off marriage proposals with his foil even as we ran to our landau."

They were both laughing with tears in their eyes now.

"My poor mother was livid, and rightfully so, not only because I was bleeding all over her drawing room, but because we'd become fodder for the broadsheets." He heaved a sigh. "I was deemed 'the Duke of Disgrace,' and it reduced our marriage prospects as well as our sisters' chances of finding a respectable match."

"I see," Camelia said.

Of course, she didn't have to tell him how reckless he had been. Just as he didn't have to explain to her how his irresponsible behavior had cast a shadow on his sisters' reputations, through no fault of their own—while they were sitting at home and working on their needlepoint, no less. As a woman, Camelia already understood society's lack of logic. London was far too confining. It sparked his ire and made him wish their time here in the Bay would never end.

That must be an unthinkable dream to her. She did not want more than this one week. He should tell Camelia now of his plans to stay, that they could have more time together, if she desired it, too. But now did not seem like the right time, when he had not yet unearthed the pain of his past.

"I should have known better, and I certainly should have known not to drag Rohan into the mess, too. My one saving grace for getting myself sliced was that Rohan didn't have a scratch on him. He has always been my mother's favorite son, as I was my father's favorite son."

Camelia ran a soothing hand up and down his arm but said nothing. He was glad she would let him get all of this out before he lost the courage to continue speaking.

"He simply smiled, asked if I was fine, then helped me clean my wound and bandage it. All without a single stern word." Raaz swallowed. "He never raised his voice. Never argued with me. Even when I *wanted* a fight. I'm sorry now I gave my father so much trouble—and my mother. I—" He exhaled a harsh breath, trying to move past the lump in his throat.

"Oh, Raaz," she murmured, kissing his shoulder.

"In my younger years, I was a nightmare to be around," Raaz said, banding his arms tightly around Camelia. "I was irascible." He gave a bitter laugh. "Even more than I am now."

"Impossible," she said with a soft laugh.

That made him laugh, too, which eased some of the tightness in his chest so he could continue.

"Why he had to leave this earth so suddenly, I'll never know. There is no answer. He was the very picture of health and vitality, even on that day, and then his heart—" Raaz's voice cracked. "Just stopped."

"Raaz, I'm so sorry," she whispered, and he felt her tears on his chest. "What an awful shock that must have been, for all of you."

"There was no reason for it," he agreed. "That's all the damned useless doctor could tell us."

"I wish it never happened," Camelia said, running her fingers through his hair.

"We found him like that, after returning home from a ball we'd attended with our mother," Raaz said. He could see it in his mind, as fresh as if it were only yesterday. "My father had wanted to stay home, pore over his charts, and read a book. That wasn't unusual for the man." Raaz cleared his throat, but what came out sounded more akin to a choked sob. "He looked so peaceful in his stuffed chair. I thought, surely, he'll snore and startle himself awake from his after-supper snooze because he remembered some astronomy paper he needed to find. I knew if I just waited one more minute, he'd wake again. Like he always did. It was a silly, childish wish."

"You are always your father's child. No matter the age. Of course you did not want to believe he was gone," Camelia said. She murmured soothing words in Gujarati and Hindi as she kissed his neck and face. "Anyone would feel the same as you did."

Raaz tightened his arms around her and pressed his face into her hair. He inhaled her scent and nuzzled the soft skin behind the shell of her ear.

"Eventually, my brother had to drag me away so we could send for the physician while my mother tried to control her own tears enough to comfort my sisters," Raaz said. "Rohan has always been more suited to being duke than I have. Without him, I would have never had the strength to sort through everything with my father's will after. Even so, my family still demanded I come here, to get away from the memory."

He'd given himself to the shadows, been consumed by them, until there was no light in his world. But shadows couldn't exist without the sun, and perhaps he'd found some of that light returned to him again. Yes. He knew it to be true because he held it in his hands right now. Raaz blinked against the hot tears that filled his eyes once more, and tucked Camelia's head under his chin so she couldn't see. He blew out a slow breath to help master his emotions. As it turned out, he couldn't quite tell her everything. He couldn't say that even more than the prospect of healing from his grief, her presence in the Bay had drawn him like a moth to flame from the moment she'd opened the door of the cottage.

He had already burdened her overmuch with his troubles. Tomorrow. He would tell her tomorrow he wanted to stay in the Bay.

CHAPTER 17

CAMELIA TOYED WITH THE END OF THE PLAIT. THE duke's large warm hands had been more deft than she'd expected. Heat had spread through her skin from his palms, massaging her scalp and neck and tugging through her hair with the perfect amount of tension. Even now, as she lay against Raaz and listened to him speak, that pulsing ache between her thighs would not subside.

The affection he so obviously held for his family had melted Camelia's heart, and the pain he recalled after the loss of his father broke it. She could imagine him plaiting his own daughter's hair one day. *Their daughter.* But she shoved the inane idea to the farthest corners of her mind so that she was not tempted to grasp dreams that would only lead to disappointment.

As they shifted to sitting up again on the sofa, it was clear from his averted eyes that Raaz needed to return to lighter conversational territory. "And who hosted this infamous house party that lasted twenty days?" Camelia asked.

"Lady Blair's parents," Raaz said, chuckling. She caught a

glint of gratitude in his warm eyes. "Doubtless they wanted their daughter married by the end of the summer. Why do you think we were so eager to get the hell out of there?"

"You all thought one of you might be next," Camelia guessed.

"Precisely," Raaz said, "and the fear was not unfounded."

"I'm certain your parents sent you there for that exact reason."

"Indeed." Raaz rolled his eyes. "Had it not been her own birthday party, Evelyn would have been the one organizing the wagers for our fencing folly and walking away with most of the winnings. But Evie had more respect for rules back then, while I had less. Now, she's become more fun over the years, and I haven't, which is sometimes the way it goes." He shrugged.

Raaz referred to Countess Blair with increasing familiarity, and although, yes, it made Camelia a fraction jealous, it mostly made her rueful. She'd been the one to believe a short-term arrangement between them would lead to *less* pain and regret. More fool her.

"I don't think her parents ever hosted a house party that lasted that long since." Raaz grinned, but there was a hint of melancholy to the expression. He still seemed lost in reminiscing as he watched the flames flicker in the hearth. The duke appeared almost as forlorn as he had on the first day he arrived at the cottage.

"I should think not." Camelia laughed. "Unless it was a success?"

"Yes, she did meet the earl that summer." Raaz smiled. "He was a better man than all of us combined."

"You and Lady Blair have known each other a long time, then?" Camelia finally asked.

"Yes," Raaz said, turning his face to her. "She and my

sisters are close in age, so they became fast friends. But we all grew up together."

"I see," Camelia said.

Unlike Raaz, she hadn't been born here, though she'd been in England long enough now that it wasn't as obvious, perhaps. But that was only on the outside. On the inside, Camelia still felt like that same lost and lonely girl who had first arrived on these shores. She wished she'd had the kind of close friendships Raaz seemed to have, both in his past, and even now with Leo and Percy. Camelia should tell him, she knew, more about her own life, especially when he had already shared so much with her. But she could not find the words to begin.

"What else do you wish to know?" he asked, misunderstanding the reason for her silence.

"How many before me?" She had not intended for the question to be quite so direct, but Raaz didn't seem to mind. In fact, he seemed to expect it, perhaps because of their conversation about Lady Blair.

"Two," he answered without hesitation.

Her shock must have been written on her face, because he huffed with amusement.

"I am by nature a recluse and not adept at social graces," he said. "Logically, it follows that I am no rake, Camelia."

"Will you tell me more?" she asked.

"If you wish." As he spoke, he absently traced his fingers over the chintz pattern of the sofa's arm. "One was a summer dalliance with the younger sister of a friend from Cambridge. It ended amicably. From the start, I never promised her anything more than that summer, so when she told me she found someone else she wanted more, it was no hardship to step out of the way."

He waited, as if to see if she was still comfortable with him continuing.

118

"And the second?" Camelia asked.

"Later, and for longer, I had an arrangement with a widow. She was a few years older than I was, and we also parted on pleasant terms."

That the duke was used to temporary arrangements of pleasure should have reassured and relieved Camelia that they could part ways with no complications when the time came.

It did not, however, make her feel better.

Raaz continued. "My life then, it was unsuitable for a wife, much less children. I was handling my responsibilities, ah, rather badly, I'm afraid. I pushed away my family and my friends, except those who were stubborn enough to refuse my attempts to oust them from my life."

"Like Leo and Percy."

"Yes, like Leo and Percy," he confirmed with a small smile, "as well as Prashant and Aarav, whom you've not met, yet."

Yet, he said, and Camelia tried not to react to that tiny word, but it was impossible not to sail away with its implied buoyancy—its silver lining. *Yet.* It promised a beautiful future beyond storm clouds. One where they might not have to leave each other.

Except she'd made them promise they would.

And her thoughts crashed back to earth with that truth.

"She—the widow—wished to marry again, and that was something I couldn't give her." Raaz said. "At the time."

Did that mean he would marry her now given half the chance? If Raaz crossed paths again with this young widow—or even someone more graceful, sophisticated, and worldly—what then? If there was someone like Lady Blair, with better standing in society—what would that mean for Camelia? It would mean nothing for her, of course, because their arrangement would be complete. A woman like her would not make a better duchess for a duke than a woman of English nobility.

A sudden crack of lightning split the sky in half and lit up

SRI SAVITA

the room, startling her from her thoughts. Thunder followed
with a sonorous, menacing rumble, and she inched closer to
Raaz on the sofa.

"Camelia," Raaz said. "Look at me. Please."

His tone was too intimate, too warm, and too gentle. She
wanted to refuse him. She wanted to run. But she could do
neither as her face turned to meet his, like a flower seeking the
sun. "Hmm?"

"I am telling you these things because you asked. I would
have anyway, because I want to be truthful with you. But I am
not the same person now that I was then. To be sure, I am not
without my flaws still, but don't interpret anything more from
my memories. They are simply that—the past. And that is all
they ever will be."

She did not know what to say to communicate how much
she understood and appreciated his forthrightness. She was
not sure she deserved so much care from him. He was not
obligated to her. They did not owe each other anything. And
she had made her own share of mistakes in the past. So, she
nodded.

"Be glad you did not know me then, for I was angrier,
more arrogant, and selfish," Raaz said with a dry laugh. "I
wasn't in a hurry to marry at the time, but . . . well, what I
mean to say is that I've matured."

If she thought his earlier frankness was more than she
could handle, then these words were even sweeter and heavier
to bear. It was a relief to know the duke had not lived his life
without reflecting on some decisions with regret, too, and that
he had grown and was different now. As she was different.
Hopefully, that meant he would understand her decisions
when she told him about her younger years as well.

"You are not going to ask me any questions?" she said.

"Anything you wish to tell me, you may, of course." Raaz

shrugged. "But your past is yours, and if you prefer your privacy, then I will respect that. I do not need to know. I can only hope I'll earn your trust someday soon."

"That is a perfect answer, Duke. One would never think you were devoid of social graces," she teased, giving his chest a playful shove.

Raaz rolled his eyes and laughed. "We'll keep this newfound knowledge to ourselves then, yes? Else I'll be fending off invitations that will arrive with a vengeance to make up for all these years away."

"I'll never tell," she agreed.

Camelia counted out the seconds of silence in the steady drumming rain. She wanted to offer Raaz something, but as much as she might dwell on the past in her own mind, she did not like to talk about it in the present. Perhaps that was because there was no one she trusted enough to listen and understand, no one with whom she could share her shame. She had not even told Binita, who had quickly become like a second mother to her.

"My experiences with men have left much to be desired," Camelia said.

"Experiences," Raaz repeated slowly. She tried not to laugh as she watched several emotions play out across his face.

"There have been two for me as well," she said. "When I was younger, in India, it was a sweeter, more innocent affair between two neighbors who'd grown up together, living side by side."

"I see," Raaz said. "And the other?"

"The second was after I arrived in England," Camelia said. "I stayed with a friend of my parents until I found work as a finishing governess. It's what I wanted to do more than anything. I enjoyed teaching painting, drawing, dancing, and music in India, and I was eager to do the same in London."

Raaz laced his fingers with hers, and she stared down at their linked hands while she continued speaking. "I did become a finishing governess, and was successful at it for quite some time. At twenty-five, I began working for a lord, who was not much older than I was and a widower. I grew quite attached to his two daughters, and they were equally fond of me." She swallowed, feeling her face burn with shame, but she had to speak the next words. "I grew quite attached to him as well."

Raaz squeezed her hand, and she squeezed back.

"Perhaps I should have known it would only spell disaster. He was nobility, and I was not. But even with our differences, I thought there was much we shared that was similar. I trusted my feelings for him were not one-sided, and I believed love could conquer any obstacles we might face."

She withdrew her hand from Raaz's and wrapped her arms around herself. "He had persuaded me of that, too, that I had brought life back to him and healed his hurt heart."

"Did he hurt you?" Raaz's voice was so intense that Camelia had to look at him. His expression was dark. Almost angry.

"Not in the way I think you mean," Camelia said, slowly. "He did not force himself on me. And I will not give you more information about him so that you can hurt him. He isn't worth that time from you."

"I'll be the judge of that," Raaz said. Then his features softened, and he muttered an oath under his breath. He took her hands in his. "He's a rotten cad."

"Yes," Camelia said, pulling her hands back and looking away. "But I only blame myself. The man I'd been with in London had promised forever, as I had promised to the man in India, and so it makes a certain kind of cruel sense that if I left one lover, another would leave me."

Raaz opened his mouth, as if to protest, but Camelia ran a soothing hand across his forearm. "Please, just let me finish."

It would be too much right now to hear soft or kind words from him when she did not believe she deserved them. It was already too much to have him here, and she was afraid of asking for more—of breaking what little they had between them now. She did not trust herself with this devastatingly handsome duke. He was here for healing, not for her—still grieving and searching for a way to connect with his father through this cottage and this village. She shouldn't keep him from that by asking for more than he was already giving.

"I left the position, because I could never work there after the humiliation of revealing my love and being met with cold silence. He claimed that what I felt was only in my mind, and the conversations we'd had and the promises we'd made were false." Her words were brittle as she forced them past the knot in her throat. She swallowed, fighting to regain some semblance of softness, because it was not the duke's fault she was still upset. She didn't want him to think her ire was directed at him. He was not the one she didn't trust. It was herself. "No one ever found out that he was my paramour, thankfully, and there were no rumors spread by him or anyone else. But I knew. And that was enough. I did not work again as a governess, and I wanted to leave London and never return."

"Camelia—"

"There's still more to tell," she said, unable to meet his eyes now. "I had to again rely on the kindness of the woman who was my parents' friend to take me back in, and she let me know I could stay as long as I liked. But I wanted to get out of Town as quickly as I could. So I grifted and gambled to scrape enough together to set out on my own again. This time for the Bay."

This was where Raaz would tell her he thought her impetuous and naive for giving up a sensible, respectable post, and disreputable for surviving the way she did afterward. A governess driven to grifting and gambling—how could that not be because of something lacking in *her*, some shortage of commitment or discipline? It seemed like Camelia's life was a series of failures and bad decisions. Perhaps she was not independent but simply alone. The two were entirely different things. Even finding herself here in the Bay, where she was finally starting to turn things right, had been by chance—all because of a game of cards.

A silent moment stretched between them. Bracing herself, Camelia lifted her eyes and met the duke's gaze.

And saw only warmth. "Camelia, please listen to me," Raaz said. "What happened to you was unfair and unkind. Of course your feelings are valid. But don't for one second believe I think of you as ruined. It would be hypocritical of me to judge your experiences when I've had my own as well."

Relief filled her. "It's probably a good thing you did not meet me when I was doing more crime than simply winning a deed from a card game," Camelia said with a laugh that sounded more like a choked sob.

"Simply? No, sweetheart." Raaz smiled, moving one hand around her back to give her plait a light tug. "I don't believe you do anything simply. You *strive*. You've left so much behind to step closer to what you want. Don't devalue your skills and efforts now. It isn't right, or even true. You haven't let that blackguard—or fear, or doubt—stop you. That is both rare and admirable."

Camelia wasn't sure what to say to that. Somehow his words both frightened her and sent something fizzing through her blood as if she had indulged in a glass of champagne. She felt, quite literally, lighter. Simultaneously unburdened and brighter. Camelia had been certain that he would judge her for how she'd had to make ends meet to live on her own. It was not, she freely admitted, perhaps the wisest or most perfect path forward. But it was the one she had forged, and it was hers alone.

Although, as she spent more time with Raaz here at the cottage, she was not sure she wanted that journey to be as lonely as it had been.

The duke stretched his arms across the back of the sofa. A softer and more wistful gleam entered his dark eyes as he looked out the window into the night. "I came here to escape London, to hide away as I sorted through my grief—to distract myself, if I'm being quite honest, by taking on the responsibility of figuring out what happened to the deed and the cottage for my father. My mother and brother were only too willing to let me ride to Robin Hood's Bay because they could see I was on a path that was dark and destructive. Perhaps they hoped time away, time spent focused on my father—on handling this one singular task—might restore me to myself." He turned his gaze back to Camelia. "And it did bring me closer to him than ever before, yes, absolutely. And for that I am glad. But I'll never think of this time as a mere detour, Camelia, most especially because it brought me to you."

Because it was always meant to be this path. Camelia bit her tongue to keep the words from slipping free past her lips. There was a better, smaller, yet altogether more powerful word for what Raaz described. Naseeb. Destiny. Fate.

In India, when Camelia was younger, her mother had taught her how to play cards. Those long evenings spent watching the sun set over the fields had inspired her love of games. There was nothing like the rush of luck finding you and the thrill of winning. Her mother had used the time to impart wisdom to her daughter as well. Camelia remembered discussing *chance* and *choice*, lofty philosophical concepts that held little importance for an impatient young girl who wanted her mother to finish dealing the cards so Camelia could play another game with her parents.

But now she understood.

Love changed everything.

"Oh, Raaz," Camelia said, warmed by his soft confession, but tears stung her eyes, and then she could say no more, or she might say too much.

CHAPTER 18

THE CANDLES BURNED LOW, AND CAMELIA SET HER empty plate next to Raaz's on the table in front of the sofa. When they'd both realized they felt a bit peckish, he'd brought bread, cheese, and raspberry jam from the larder for them to eat.

"The man in India that I mentioned," she said. "I was engaged to him."

Raaz turned to her but said nothing, only laid his hand atop her thigh. Camelia drew strength from the comforting heat of his touch as it warmed her skin through the silk of the dressing gown she wore. His dressing gown. It was an exquisite shade of Sardinian blue, like a tranquil summer sea or sky. But if Camelia felt calm as she divulged her past, she knew it was not because of the beautiful raiment that embraced her. Her peace was entirely due to the man beside her.

"What happened to end your engagement?" Raaz asked, the same thunderous look in his eyes as before.

"Nothing drastic, and no, he did not hurt me, either," she reassured him. "But still, I could not marry him when the day finally came. I'd committed too quickly. Despite growing up next door to each other, we knew nothing about each other. Not about the things that mattered, anyway. In good conscience, I could not go through with it. I came to England to start over, and then, as fate would have it, I had to leave London for the same reason to come to the Bay. My parents understood my reasons for leaving home after the wedding was called off, but it did not make the decision, or the distance, any easier—for anyone. I try to send my parents letters when I can so they know I'm well, and they write to me, too."

A surge of homesickness overwhelmed Camelia, and she closed her eyes.

"Camelia, sweetheart," Raaz said, stroking her thigh gently. "Come back to me. What is it?"

She opened her eyes. "I've known you for less time than the man I was affianced to, and my lover in London was a lord. Neither of those turned out well," Camelia said, biting her lower lip. "It was enough to make me avoid any such entanglements forever." She stared at his hand for a moment before lifting her eyes to meet his. "Or so I thought, until now."

"Well, look who also has perfect, pretty words," Raaz murmured. "I *like* that you go after what you want—that you take risks. I came here to sequester. But you came here to start again, and—" He hesitated. "I'm sorry if it took an unkind world to make it that way, sweetheart. I wish it didn't have to be. But you're the bravest person I know, Camelia, and I know I'm better for having met you."

"I feel the same," Camelia said, "for knowing you, Raaz. I've never shared that much about my life with anyone before. Ever. Thank you for listening, for understanding, and for helping me feel less alone."

The duke leaned forward and pressed his lips to the corner of her mouth, then moved her plait to the opposite shoulder to kiss the back of her neck. "We ought to be rewarded for our candor, don't you think?" he said against her skin.

"Yes," Camelia breathed.

Raaz took her by the hand and pulled her to the corner of the room until they stood before the long cheval glass. To their right were the windows. To their left were the two sofas and the low table. They'd been sitting on one sofa moments ago and had their first kiss when they played cards on the other. Directly behind them was the bed they'd slept in together. And, of course, there was the copper bathtub.

Camelia had too many memories here with the duke already, in such a short time. And that was only in this one single room. But their week of passion and pleasure was not over, and she did not have to let go yet. They still had all night together, and she wanted to make every minute count.

It was as if they both had the same thought at the same time, born out of the desire and desperation to remain in the present. Camelia and Raaz reached for each other with the storm still raging all around them outside. She craved only feeling, only sensation, as she glided her hands down the silk of his banyan until she found the belt, eager to have his warm skin against hers. But before she could undress him, he stopped her.

"You first," Raaz whispered to her in the dim firelight, and turned her to face the mirror. He untied the belt of her dressing gown, slid the silk from around her shoulders, and tossed it onto the back of a chair. "Watch yourself in the mirror, Camelia."

She did as the duke bade, shivering at both the seductive command and the contact of his palms on her skin. His large, warm hands were calloused from working on the cottage. Raaz dragged his touch over her breasts, mapping each curve and traveling down to the dip of her waist. He left one hand there, and he curled the other around her neck, pushing upward to expose the underside of her jaw. Their gazes locked in the looking glass, and the heat of his breath set her flushed skin on fire.

"Raaz," she gasped, turning to meet his mouth with hers.

He ducked his head and laughed against her skin. "No. Not yet. I want you to see every second of this."

There was the slightest touch of his lips at the hinge of her jaw before the hand at her waist snaked even lower. When he reached the triangle of dark curls between her thighs, he parted her slick folds with two thick fingers. She arched against his chest, further exposing the column of her throat to him. He hummed with appreciation, and her pulse thrummed with the feel of his voice against her skin. His whiskers scraped her skin as he nuzzled her neck. The duke grazed his teeth along her pulse as he circled the bundle of nerves where she desired his attention the most. Camelia whimpered and fought to swallow against the sudden dryness in her throat. This teasing was too much to bear, and it was difficult to find air to breathe when she was burning. She closed her eyes to focus on the sensations. But then Raaz's fingers moved away.

"Open your eyes, Camelia." The words were a low, hypnotic caress she was helpless to resist. "Look at me. Or I'll stop."

Camelia's eyes flew open to find that his intent, simmering gaze was trained on hers. Raaz looked like she felt—caught in the same haze of lust that made everything go soft around the edges. Camelia drove her hips closer to him as he pressed into her back. *Ah.* Mercifully, not *everything* was soft. She could find relief like this, grinding against him, if he'd only let her. But he dropped the hand at her throat down to her hip and held her in place, and it was all simultaneously moving too fast and too slow.

Instead of continuing to circle between her legs, Raaz brought his other hand up to cup her jaw and dragged his thumb across her lower lip. Camelia caught it between her teeth and traced the tip of it with her tongue.

"Fuck," he hissed. His shallow, heavy breaths were as broken as hers, and his eyes were liquid pools of black. Raaz's tousled hair fell over his forehead, and Camelia reached up behind her to twine her arms around his neck. Keeping his grip on her waist, he lowered his hand again and resumed those small, tight, tormenting circles with the pad of his thumb—the same thumb that she had just licked.

Everything inside her was ablaze with fever and attuned to the thrum of desire as it moved lower. Her quim ached with need. She was desperate, waiting for more. Waiting to be filled —with his fingers, with his cock. Her eyes fell closed again, and she squeezed them tighter, trying to focus only on sensation and not the worries of what might happen if she were to let him spill inside her. In truth, she did not abhor the idea of a child, especially not one with the duke. It was tempting to give in to that wish, but that would be unwise for so many reasons. When it came to that, she would ask Wednesbury to withdraw. It was safer that way, for both of them.

"I can't," she whined. "It's too much."

"I assure you, it isn't. I know you can take more, darling," Raaz said with an amused laugh. "My fingers aren't even inside you yet, and you won't get them if I have to ask you to pay attention again."

She met his eyes in the mirror. "Please," she begged. She tried to move her hips against his hand, craving the friction, searching for something—*anything*—to ease this ache.

"Patience," he said. "Let me enjoy how drenched you are —how charmingly responsive and so very eager. Tell me, Camelia, is it always like this?"

"No. Only with you," she admitted, and was satisfied when that shattered Raaz's sangfroid. He groaned against her neck.

"Look at us," he said, and they both watched in the glass as he finally dipped one finger inside her. Camelia cried out, and Raaz captured the sound with a deep, unhurried kiss that had her writhing against his hand. He broke away, panting. "God, you're already dripping down my wrist, but I won't make this easy for you. I'm going to take my time with you tonight."

Moonlight and lightning from the windows haloed them both with a soft, silvery glow. Raaz curled one finger inside her. Camelia's lips parted, and she moaned before she realized the sound was coming from her. Raaz squeezed her breasts with his free hand. Her nipples were tight, dark points of need, and he toyed with each for only a few brief, infuriating moments before ignoring them and returning his free hand to grip her waist, holding her against the hard heat of his erection.

"Touch yourself, love," the duke said, pumping his finger in time with the circles around her clitoris. "Let me watch you like you're watching me."

She pinched and rolled her nipples, arching against him and sighing his name. "More," she pleaded. "I need more from you."

"Can you handle another finger, Camelia?" Raaz asked.

"Yes," she whimpered, looking at his eyes in the mirror as he slid one more thick finger inside her cunt. Her muscles tightened around him as the first tremor tore through her, and this time they both moaned. Thunder still rumbled in the distance and rain clinked against the glass, but for a few moments there were only the erotic, wet sounds of sex and their panting sighs that filled the room.

"Will you take one more, sweetheart?" Raaz murmured. "For me, please."

"You can try," Camelia whispered, and he added another finger. With three fingers, she was so full he hardly had to move at all before she was trembling. A mess of broken words spilled from her lips in between sighs and moans as she begged for more. Finally, she found relief, and wave after wave of pleasure flooded her body and pooled between her legs.

"That's it. Breathe," Raaz coaxed soothingly, his fingers still inside her. "Show me how much you need this. Be as loud as you want, love. There's no one here but us."

When at last her release had subsided, Camelia's knees almost buckled, and she leaned against the duke to avoid sliding to the floor in a puddle. She turned in his arms and tugged at his banyan, trying to climb closer, seeking his lips, wanting him to crush his mouth to hers. Hard.

"Easy, easy. Shh, I know," Raaz said. He settled his mouth over hers, soothing her with long, lush kisses. The duke lifted her, and she wrapped her legs around his waist as he carried her to the sofa.

"You've been so good," he said, setting her on the cushions. He sank down to his knees and settled between hers. "Now open for me and give me more. Let me take care of you."

Camelia did as he asked, and Raaz's fingers traced through her slick arousal as he found that sensitive spot and circled it again.

"Wait." She clutched his shoulders, and panic made her nails dig into the silk.

"I didn't know you enjoyed delaying gratification," the duke said with a dark laugh. "I'm happy to help keep you on the edge. Just say the word."

"No, that's not—" Camelia said, even more flustered now. "What?"

"Let's come back to that later," Raaz said with a smile. "I think you may enjoy it with me." His tongue darted out to wet his lips.

Yes, she was sure she would enjoy anything with him.

SRI SAVITA

Camelia dragged her hands through his hair and said, "I have to tell you something."

Raaz kept his eyes on hers as he sucked his fingers into his mouth and licked them clean. Without appearing to think twice. As if it were the most natural thing in the world to do. Like he had no idea that she had burst into flames with that one single, small gesture. Or, judging by the slight quirk to the corner of his lips, perhaps he did know what effect he had on her and had done it on purpose. Camelia struggled to recover her thoughts about what she wanted to say as he rose and sat beside her on the sofa.

"What is it?" he asked, studying her face. "Have you had enough?"

"No," Camelia reassured him, placing a palm on his forearm. "But I've never experienced this. That is to say, I've never had anyone do this before—taste me." The last two words were a barely audible whisper, and she hated that heat rose to her cheeks. "In case that changes anything for you."

"As you saw, I've already tasted you," Raaz said with a wicked smile. "So, thank you for sharing, but this changes nothing for me, except that I want to do it even more now."

"I see," Camelia managed to say, but the words were tight.

Raaz's brows knit together with concern. "Does it change anything for you? If there's something I should or shouldn't do, then tell me. But I want to taste you—and I *need* to," he said.

Camelia nodded and swallowed, too stunned by the force of his request to speak.

"Give me your words, Camelia," he said gruffly, tipping her chin toward him.

"Yes," she said. "Please."

"That's my sweet girl," the duke said.

He knelt on the carpet again and spread her legs. Raaz lightly bit the sensitive skin on the inside of her thigh, then licked over it before kissing her other thigh in the same manner. The rough scrape of his whiskers against her skin reignited that fire within her.

"I'm done talking, Camelia. All I want to do now is sip from you until I'm drunk on your taste. Since you've shared your secrets, perhaps you can open for me now, too, and enjoy this."

He glanced up at her, eyes soft with lust, waiting for her to object. "That sounds fine," Camelia whispered.

Raaz chuckled against her skin, and the gust of warm breath made her gasp. "By the end of this, sweetheart, I hope *fine* is not what I walk away with from you."

Camelia wanted to amend her words right then as Raaz licked between her folds.

"Raaz," she said with a sharp gasp, twining her fingers more tightly into his hair.

He was soft and tentative at first, flicking the tip of his tongue against her clitoris. He was giving her time to adjust to the sensation, but she whimpered and moved against his mouth to tell him that she needed more pressure. Everywhere.

Raaz gave a deep sound of satisfaction, and she felt the rumble of it climb up her body and elicit another cry from her throat. The duke tasted her with increasingly firm, eager, and urgent swipes of his tongue. When he dipped inside her soaked channel, as if it were his cock and not his tongue thrusting, her orgasm tore through her with a rush of wet heat.

"Please," Camelia begged, unsure of what she was pleading for—for him to continue or stop. Both seemed like torment of the sweetest kind.

Raaz broke away, replacing his tongue with his fingers. "Yes. That's it, my love. Let me have it," Raaz said, and curved his fingers inside her. "There's no need to be quiet. We're the only ones here. Give me every last sound and wave. Let me have all of you."

He returned his mouth to her clitoris and hummed with appreciation, which only heightened the pleasure of what his mouth and fingers were doing to her quim. She tangled her fingers into his hair, holding on to him, as he held her hips against his lips. Camelia had the sense that as he lost himself in her, he wished to surround himself with her, that he wasn't seeking escape so much as refuge. That she could be a kind of sanctuary for him, even if only for a little while longer, brought tears to her eyes yet again.

CHAPTER 19

RAAZ DIDN'T REMEMBER FALLING ASLEEP THE NIGHT before, but he dreamed he was still tasting Camelia. When he woke, she was breathing deeply in sleep. Though he was loath to leave the bed, he resisted the urge to kiss her and disturb her sleep, and he instead went into his room to complete his morning ablutions and change into fresh clothes from his portmanteau.

The dawn was bright and clear with nary a cloud in the sky. Sunlight painted the horizon with a pretty blush, not unlike the hue he'd ignited all over Camelia's skin the night before. Raaz grinned, despite the treacly sentiment. A walk to The Bay Blossom in the cool morning air and a cup of masala chai ought to start the day right.

Despite how quickly the summer storm had passed, he hoped last night's rain would slow progress on the remaining repairs to the stable's roof. With any luck, he and Camelia might now have more than the one week together they'd agreed upon.

But as Raaz trekked through the fields to get down the hill to the inn, his heart sank. The ground wasn't too muddy, and if the sun continued to steadily shine throughout the day, they'd be able to get back to work on the roof without too much delay.

No matter. He would approach with a different strategy. Raaz would tell Camelia of his plans to build on the land surrounding the cottage to gauge how his desire to stay longer in the Bay would be received. He could take her to see the spot he had picked out for building the glasshouse, and he would show her sketches of his plans. They could make a day of it. Yes, that was a fine idea. If the weather was not going to help him, then he would take advantage of the sun. He'd get enough food to pack a basket. It was a beautiful day to have a picnic by the lake he'd found within a small, secluded circle of trees. He'd lay a blanket down over the grass, and he and Camelia could have an encore performance of last night's filthy events for the flora and fauna. In his mind, she wore a crown of flowers and nothing else for the rest of the afternoon as the sunlight shimmered on her warm gold skin. Hell, he'd wear a coronet of ivy and thorns and prance around in the nude, too, for all he cared. They could even take a dip in the lake naked. He'd do whatever Camelia pleased, if it meant he could have his fae queen all to himself.

CAMELIA CAME DOWNSTAIRS AND WAS GREETED BY the sight of Raaz sitting at a table in the drawing room with a tea tray and the newspaper, reading intently. With spectacles. The cat slept curled up in the chair opposite Raaz, which was as much a ringing endorsement of Camelia's inkling that Billi liked the duke as one could get from a feline. Her fingers curled into fists at her sides, because she was tempted to squeeze both Raaz and the cat in an embrace so tight they'd both surely claw her face clean off. Trying to approach in a way that would not startle or interrupt him from his reading, she took the seat to Raaz's left.

"Good morning," he said, turning to her and setting aside the paper. He slid a small plate of pastries toward her with a wicked, smug glint in his eyes. "I know today's your day off, and I thought you might want to sleep later than usual. You must be hungry. Eat."

Camelia's cheeks heated, both from the ribald reminder of last night and the knowledge that he must have gone to The Bay Blossom very early in the morning to get these raspberry pastries before they sold out. She knew these had quickly become the duke's favorite, and had it not been her day off, she would have been the one baking them instead of Binita, and bringing some extra home to him.

"You wear spectacles?" Camelia asked, and even though she was pleased she'd learned the duke's preference for pastries in such a short time, this reminded her there were still things they did not know about each other. That was suddenly easy to forget. Last night had been wonderful in many ways, not the least of which being how they had shared the secrets of their pasts and grown closer in the process.

So close that, as the duke's tongue darted out to collect a dab of jam from the corner of his mouth, she recalled the way his tongue had dipped into her quim in much the same way. Camelia pressed her thighs together and pretended to smooth her skirts.

At her question, Raaz reached up to adjust the frames. He seemed to only now have remembered they were still on his face, and he looked a bit embarrassed.

"Ah, yes. For reading," he admitted, and ducked his head to remove them.

Camelia stayed his hand. "Leave them on," she said.

"It's easier if I take them off for this," he murmured, pulling her into his lap.

"Fine, but I'll do it." Camelia lifted the spectacles from his face and set them on the table before leaning in to kiss him.

When they finally broke apart for a breath, Raaz said, "All right, enough of this, or we'll never leave the house." He dragged his dark gaze over her celestial blue morning walking dress, which had delicate gold embroidery and glass beading. "Will you be comfortable riding in these pretty clothes?"

"I suppose that depends on what I'm riding," Camelia said. She lifted her skirts made from sari silk and turned to straddle his lap, circling her arms around his neck.

"Your mount, damn you," Raaz said with a laugh.

Camelia arched a brow and smiled with feigned inno-cence. "I'm sorry, Your Grace, but that still doesn't clarify."

"You know perfectly well I'm referring to your horse," Raaz said, even as he wrapped his arms more tightly around her waist and pulled her closer. "We're taking Pavan and Shandar and touring the grounds. I even packed a picnic with Binita's assistance. You wouldn't want to let all that go to waste now, would you? Think of how poor Binita will feel. It was more her effort than mine, which I'm sure comes as no surprise."

Regardless of Binita's involvement, it warmed her heart that he had thought to plan all this.

"Binita said there's no reason to worry. Even with the festival beginning soon, she can spare you," Raaz said with a grin. "And I won't keep you out too late. Nothing would give me greater pleasure than to make sure we're both in bed by dusk."

"No doubt that's true," Camelia said dryly, but she was just as eager to fall back into bed with him and draw the covers over their heads. Just the two of them in their own little world. But cotton linens weren't strong enough to keep out the reality of their dwindling time together, so Camelia meant to enjoy today to the fullest with the duke.

"Pavan and I will race you and Shandar down to the beach," Camelia said. She kissed the corner of his mouth and hopped down from his lap as gracefully as she could manage, then pranced out of the drawing room.

"That's cheating," Raaz exclaimed, and she heard the legs of his chair scrape against the floor as he presumably rose to give chase. He was close behind as she dashed up the stairs to change, and he shouted after her, "You didn't allow us to start at the same time."

"Oh, don't be a sore loser, Your Grace," Camelia called over her shoulder.

"I won't," he said with a laugh. "Because you haven't won yet."

CHAPTER 20

Camelia guided Pavan down the path to the shore. Stony cliffs stood like sentinels in the background, and she turned in her saddle to see Raaz and Shandar approaching.

"Again," Raaz said, when he'd brought his black mount to a stop beside Camelia and her buckskin gelding. "And to ensure we have the same advantage, I insist we start together."

"I see you are indeed a sore loser, Your Grace," Camelia said with a laugh.

"Not so," Raaz said, scowling, but it quickly softened into a grin. "But I'll have none of your tempting tricks to distract me this time, darling. So don't even try it."

"A wild accusation," Camelia said. "In fact, you should have arrived earlier than me, as I had to change into my riding habit."

"Well," Raaz drawled, "What kind of gentleman would I be if I let you do it alone?"

She lifted one shoulder. "I'm sure I would have managed without your, ah, rather enthusiastic *help*."

"Yes, but would it have been as enjoyable?" He grinned.

Camelia laughed. "Fine, I agree to your terms. Only, let's give the horses a rest first."

Their horses walked side by side along the shoreline. Sunlight sparkled over the waves, and Camelia watched the water kiss the sand before pulling pebbles out to tumble with it again. The breeze blew a few tendrils of her hair loose from under her hat, and she gathered her reins in one gloved hand before trying to tuck the long strands behind her ear.

"Here," Raaz said, trying not to smile at her uncoordinated struggle. He nudged Shandar closer and gently brushed the hair from her cheek. "Do you think the horses have rested enough now?"

Camelia didn't wait to give him an answer and instead urged Pavan into a canter along the beach.

"Miss Parikh," Raaz called after her with a laugh. "This is most unsporting of you, and you don't even know where we're going next."

Her laughter was swept away by the breeze as she and Pavan made their way up the hills to the longer grasses. When Camelia reached the top, she took in the view of the entire Bay stretching out before her, clear and crystalline blue.

"Beautiful, isn't it?" Raaz said, when he'd joined her.

Camelia looked away from the craggy coast to take in the strong lines and sharp angles of his profile. "Yes," she said.

He turned to meet her gaze, searching her face for a moment and giving her a curious look. "Shall we?" he said, leading Shandar to walk ahead of Pavan.

The duke described the crops he'd discussed planting with the tenant farmers in keeping with the four-field rotation, and Camelia asked what Leo and Percy's plans were for their time in the Bay, other than getting into mischief, of course. Soon they came to a quiet corner of the land that overlooked the rolling green farmland on one side, the cliffs and the Bay on the other.

"This is the best place to watch the sunlight in the morning," Raaz said.

"Perfect for a glasshouse, then," Camelia added.

The duke met her eyes with a surprised expression. "Yes, that's exactly what I was thinking."

She smiled, pleased to know how much he'd appreciate such a space. He could cultivate his plants and flowers and perfect his botanical sketches here.

There was room to grow and expand. If he stayed in the Bay.

She saw the picture so clearly in her mind.

His gaze on her face was as warm as the sunshine. "And perhaps a painting studio beside the glasshouse as well," he said.

Against her better judgment, Camelia felt the small, beating wings of hope taking flight. Even though she knew these were only discussions of dreams that would vanish before they became reality.

"Perfect," she said. Because it did indeed sound that way. And because she could not safely say more, else that butterfly in her stomach would be freed. It was beautiful enough to be here, with Raaz, and that the duke knew her so well was already more than she ought to have of him or his time. But as she listened to his plans for the gardens, and for the other buildings in the Bay that were part of the estate, she reminded herself that Raaz might have said he didn't think her ruined, but that did not mean he loved her. And even if he did, he had not promised marriage.

They dismounted and collected their bags and the picnic basket to let the horses graze, then walked through the wooded path to the pond Raaz had found. The trees formed a canopy of green that seemed to transport them to another world, and Camelia studied the changing shadows and light with great interest, grateful she had remembered to pack her painting supplies and easel. When they emerged from the shaded forest into a sunny glade, she helped Raaz arrange the blanket on the grass. They ate sandwiches and sipped chai in companionable silence, watching the pond.

After their picnic, Raaz moved the blanket and leaned back against the trunk of a tree. He pulled his leather-bound journal and pencil from his bag and began to write. Camelia watched him for a bit. It was impossible not to—he was striking when he was so deep in thought. She thought again of him tasting her. He'd worn a similar expression on his face then. She knew what it felt like to have the full focus of Raaz's intense attention turned on her, and so she appreciated his serious care and regard even more now.

Camelia was curious as to whether the longer strokes of his pencil meant that he was sketching, too. She wanted to see what his artist's eye observed compared to her own. Did she and the duke see the world similarly despite their differences in station? Or differently despite their similarities in artistic interests? Did she truly want the answer when their paths were destined to diverge no matter what?

She sighed, gathered her paintbox and easel, and set up closer to the pond so she could capture the landscape en plein air. It was a quiet, slow, peaceful day, as if the hours stretched languidly in the sun, too, not in any hurry to leave, and Camelia was grateful for it. Every now and then, she'd slide her gaze toward the duke. When he finally set down his journal and pencil and closed his eyes for a nap, she breathed a sigh of relief and pulled two of her calling cards from her bag. She'd started painting these cards several days ago when Raaz had been visiting the tenant farms.

It was too sentimental of her to presume he might want some reminder of their time together here, or her, before they parted ways. In fact, it was the exact opposite of what she'd proposed with their temporary arrangement. She'd insisted on no attachments after the time it took to repair the stable roof. About a week, and then they'd part. Nevertheless, she'd changed her mind and wanted to give him a parting gift.

As a reminder of the card games that won her the cottage's deed and her first kiss with Raaz, Camelia had fashioned each calling card into a playing card–style portrait. She depicted herself as the Queen of Hearts, and the duke as the King of Hearts. All that remained were some embroidery and beading details in the sari pallu draped over her head and shoulders, the mehndi on her hands, and the jewel in the pagdi that Raaz wore on his head.

Once Camelia was done adding in those colors and designs, she let the paintings dry on the easel, grateful for the light breeze and warm sunshine that would make quick work of it today. She could put the cards back into her bag before Raaz woke from his doze and ruined the surprise.

RAAZ WOKE WITH A START AND REALIZED HE'D nodded off in the comforting, cool shade of the tree. He was enjoying their day in the sun, and they both deserved an afternoon of lightness after the tumult of emotions that had poured out between them the night before, a storm within the storm.

"That's quite good," Raaz said, coming up behind Camelia as she stepped back to assess her canvas.

"Don't sound so surprised, Your Grace," Camelia said dryly.

"That isn't how I meant it," Raaz murmured, wrapping his arms around her waist and dropping a kiss on her shoulder. He stayed like that behind her, with his chin resting near her collarbone. He pointed to a corner of the painting. "I like what you've done with the light and shading. Especially here, with the entrance of the wooded path leading into the clearing. The tall grass, the insects, the pond, and the ducks. It all looks so soft. Magical, even."

Like the start to a fairy tale in an enchanted forest. The kind of start to a fairy-tale life he wanted with her in the Bay. But first he had to tell her that he wanted to stay, and Raaz had not found the courage to do that yet. He did not want to risk ruining this perfect day with her.

"Thank you," Camelia said, blushing again.

"Come here," Raaz said, taking her by the hand and pulling her toward the blanket. "I have an idea."

"What is it?" Camelia asked.

"Sit across from me," Raaz said, tucking his pencil behind his ear. He tore a page from his journal and passed it to her along with another pencil. Then he handed her a book so she could keep her paper on a sturdy surface while she sketched. "Let's have another race, but this time we'll sketch each other."

"Dueling portraits," Camelia said with a laugh. "I like it."

"I thought you might," Raaz said, pleased he could coax a smile to her face with the prospect of competition. He liked knowing such things about her. "But this time, I'll start us both."

"You don't trust me to do it, Duke?" she asked with a coy smile.

"No." Raaz snorted and took his own pencil in hand. "Ready?"

"Ready," she answered.

"Begin," he said.

"Are we evaluating each other on how well the portraits resemble our likeness?" she asked as she sketched. "Or additional creative details, such as the pond in the background?"

"You may sketch whatever else you wish, but the portrait must be there, and it must be the focus of the scene," Raaz said with a smile. "Those are the only rules. Other than to be quiet, as you're distracting me and moving your face and body too much for me to get this down on paper correctly."

"Fine," Camelia said.

They furiously moved their hands across their pages in the silence. Occasionally, their eyes would meet as they both looked up to study the other's features for their respective drawings. They'd give each other bewildering, shy smiles, and it damned well felt like he was courting her. But that wasn't what was happening here, according to Camelia, and it was best not to get confused.

Hell and damnation, she'd said only one week of pleasure, and he'd already lost his wits after just one night. Raaz had not wanted to overwhelm Camelia the first time his face was between her thighs—hadn't wanted to push for more than she was willing to give. It would have been deuced difficult to withdraw last night, even when he knew the restraint was necessary to protect her and himself. So it was a bloody relief when she had not wanted to go any further—doubly so, because if Raaz had been inside Camelia, then he would not have half the sense he was only barely managing to grasp onto today.

So instead of staring at her endlessly, Raaz trained his gaze on his journal and pencil.

"Done," Camelia said. "I win."

"Certainly not," Raaz scoffed. "Let's see them first. And mine obviously took longer. I had to work from memory because I drew you nude."

And he'd been distracted by the real-life woman in front of him. The one he wanted to keep even more than the sketch he'd done of her.

"I had to work from memory, too, Your Grace," Camelia said, rolling her eyes. "Easy enough."

"Oh, *easy*, was it?" He laughed. "Then I must've made quite the impression last night."

She gave an amused huff and revealed her drawing to Raaz. He tossed his sketchbook and pencil aside before pulling her down on the blanket for a kiss.

"No one's ever captured me in quite so much detail," he said with a grin. "It would seem, then, that I'm immensely memorable."

"I may have exaggerated some of your proportions," Camelia said, breathless, with a nonchalant shrug against the blanket.

"Cheeky minx. No, I think you got them all exactly right," he said. "I must say, I make a very flattering subject."

"Clearly I forgot to make your head significantly larger, Your Grace," Camelia teased as she watched him preen.

God, how he loved this woman. He loved her, and yet, she wanted him to leave and return to London. Well, no, that wasn't quite right. She seemed to think it had to be this way. Because she did not think she could be his duchess. That the divide between them was too vast. Very well then, he would cross it and come to her. He would make his life in the Bay. And when she was ready, he would ask if she wanted to join his life with hers, and then they could marry.

"Next time, we'll use paint," Camelia said.

"Deal," Raaz said, propping his head up on one elbow. He had a few ideas of exactly what they could do with it, too, but before he could share any of them, there was a rustling near the pond. Something made a loud yelp, followed by a splash in the water.

He turned behind him to look. "What—"

"It's a puppy," Camelia answered, bolting to her feet. "I believe it might be hurt and have fallen into the pond."

Raaz stood and ran after her before she jumped into the pond to retrieve the poor creature. He caught her arm and pulled her back from where she was peering over the water's edge, trying to find where the pup had gone.

"Careful you don't fall in, too," Raaz said.

"Oh, Raaz, I think it went there to hide," Camelia said, shaking free of his grasp and pointing toward a mossy log that had sprouted some toadstools.

"Stay here," Raaz said, shrugging out of his jacket and waistcoat. Camelia held them while he waded to the marshy, shallow area. "And mind your skirts. There's too much muck here."

CHAPTER 21

"NOT ONE WORD OUT OF YOU," RAAZ GRUMBLED, AS he trudged up to the cottage soaked through with mud for the second time in as many days.

Camelia ducked her head and covered her mouth with one hand to hide her laughter. When she'd regained her composure enough to speak, she said, "Yes, of course, Your Grace. Not a single word about this to anyone."

"As for you, let's wash this pond scum off," Raaz said in a gruff tone to the bundle of fluff wrapped in his jacket. "Outside."

Camelia handed Raaz toweling from the line. While he went to get the pup cleaned up, she took advantage of the time to return her paints and easel back to her room. Camelia washed up, too, then changed out of her riding habit and back into the celestial blue morning walking dress she'd worn earlier.

When she went downstairs, Camelia found Raaz on the Chesterfield in the library, dressed in fresh clothes and warming himself by the hearth with his feet propped up on a table. His eyes were closed, yet he once again wore his spectacles. The now clean Scotch collie puppy lay to one side of the duke, and the black and white cat was curled up on the other. There was, of course, ample seating in the library. Another sofa was directly across from the one Raaz occupied, and two more wingback chairs were set on opposite sides to form a square of furniture around the low table in the center.

But the fact that all three beasts had chosen to slumber together peacefully on the same sofa made Camelia's heart so full of joy and light and other soft emotions that she felt like it was going to burst if she did not squeal or scream. She wanted to squeeze all three of them but didn't dare risk waking them.

Camelia resisted the desire and tried to find a place where she could leave the Queen of Hearts portrait for the duke to discover later.

She walked past the gleaming, dark wooden bookshelves stocked with thick volumes, and though she longed to run her fingers over the spines, she didn't have time to read right now. She had to hide the portrait before the duke woke. The matching mahogany desk, large and handsome in front of the arched window, ought to be the perfect place. She went behind the desk and debated between the drawers, but suddenly, the sunlight streaming in from the window behind her illuminated a journal amid the ledgers and books haphazardly stacked across the surface.

Its hand-tooled leather cover helped her recognize it was the same book Raaz had been sketching in at the pond. It would make the perfect hiding place for her portrait card. Camelia inched closer to the edge of the desk.

Sketches of a regal badger bedecked with a crown and cloak spilled across the pages. Basil was drawn from various angles with different expressions. There was also a cat in a tailcoat holding a quizzing glass and reading a newspaper, obviously meant to evoke Billi's debonair persona, and on the next page were two horses in top hats that bore a strong resemblance to Shandar and Pavan.

Curious, she turned to the next page. There were more characters here than the ones Raaz had drawn from their life. A fox wearing a shirt, braces, and trousers was painting with watercolors at an easel like hers. Beneath that fine fellow were ducks wearing waistcoats and holding hands of cards between their feathers. A stoat and a rabbit—both sporting smart cravats—sat down to tackle a tower of raspberry mille-feuille together. There were three sheep in bonnets using their own wool to knit, and two puppies playing pall-mall, one named Pepper and the other—well, she couldn't quite read the duke's handwriting there.

Camelia turned the page again and finally found what she was searching for—a goat adorned with a coronet of wildflowers and munching on apple slices that could be none other than Bakri. She couldn't hold back her smile. It seemed His Grace and the troublemaking goat had finally become friends.

Snippets of writing were crammed in between the drawings, and they were all about the hijinks and adventures they'd had with the animals at the cottage, as well as some new stories. And there, hastily scribbled into one bent corner of a page, was a title to corral these creative creatures. *King Basil of the Bay.* This was followed by a question mark, as if the duke had needed to write quickly to capture the idea before it left him but wasn't quite sure he wanted to commit to it.

She turned the page again. Here were notes on the progress of the stable roof repairs, the plants in the garden, and sketched plans for the glasshouse and painting studio they'd discussed today. Entranced by his sketches and detailed plans, she read further, until one passage arrested her progress.

My mother, sisters, and brother all wish for me to marry and begin a family of my own. Soon, they will meet Camelia. I wonder what they will think . . .

Her delight at Raaz's drawings turned to ash in moments. Camelia couldn't make out the rest of the sketches and words because her vision had blurred. Dismay and guilt tangled inside her—dismay at what these words must mean, and guilt for reading thoughts not meant for her eyes.

Her desire to spend longer than just this one week of pleasure with the duke was selfish and shortsighted. She couldn't be what stood in the way of him starting a family. While Raaz might not think her ruined, he could never truly entertain the idea of marriage with her. His family, especially his mother, would surely expect more from a duchess. Perhaps Camelia had played the part well enough these past few days, at least in appearance, by wearing dresses and gloves and speaking of intimacy with the duke. But his family would want something—someone—real. And no doubt, so would the duke.

Raaz stirred in his sleep. Blinking away tears, Camelia looked up in time to watch him curl his arms around both the puppy and cat as though he thought they might slide off the edge of the sofa. Her heart gave another squeeze at that. Before Raaz could notice, or she could second-guess the wisdom in doing so, she borrowed his pencil from the cup on the desk and scrawled a note on the back of her portrait. Then she tucked it between the pages of his journal and closed the cover to keep the card safe inside. "Camelia?" Raaz's voice was low, warm, and sleepy. Her face was scarlet with heat, she was certain. The duke made a deep groaning sound as he stretched his long limbs, and even with her tangled emotions, she felt an answering flutter in her core. Now, she flushed for entirely different reasons.

"I'm sorry," she said, walking over to him. "I wasn't—it

was just—well, you left it open. And I know that's no excuse, but you see, I didn't mean to pry."

"Hush, it's all right," Raaz said with a soft laugh, pulling her down onto his lap. "Not to worry. I don't mind. In fact, I was going to show you anyway. Eventually." He sighed and dragged a hand through his hair, somehow and very unfairly making it more disheveled and more adorable at the same time. "But then, well, these are only silly little scribbles, nothing like your impressive oil paintings, and I reconsidered sharing them."

He assumed she had only seen his drawings. She would not dispel him of that notion, if only because she was a coward and still wanted him to look upon her with kindness.

Camelia pushed aside her sadness for now, concerned by the duke's deprecating words. She shouldn't have been so prideful at the pond and bristled when he said her painting was *quite good*. The duke had wanted to connect with her through something she had a passion for. And what had she wanted to do? Win their dueling portrait competition to show she was equal to him—*no*, to show she was better. To prove she would be just fine without him when he returned to London. She'd forgotten winning was lonely—there could only be one champion, after all. But all was not lost. She could try to make up for the damage she might have done.

"You should finish writing the stories, Your Grace," she said, "and you should share them—with more than just me."

"Perhaps," the duke said, but he didn't seem convinced. "At the very least," he continued, "my future children might enjoy them for a while, until they're old enough not to want to spend time with their father and his fanciful characters anymore."

Camelia looked out the window again as her sadness resurfaced. The hopes for children. An *heir* he wouldn't be having with her. And this was precisely why she was so torn, why she

155

couldn't ask Raaz to stay. He should be finding that future duchess and starting on that family. Not wasting time with her.

"I should go." She moved off his lap. "I apologize for disrupting your rest."

"Don't leave," he said, catching her by the wrist and standing, too. "I don't want you to go."

Camelia didn't want to pretend that he was asking for more than just today from her, but the way he looked right now, so warm and rumpled, and the way he looked at her, so soft and tender, was too much to bear. Taking advantage of her hesitation, Raaz leaned closer, but before their lips could meet, the puppy barked and the cat meowed, and both animals dashed from the sofa into the adjoining study.

"Raspberry," the duke said with an exasperated sigh. He followed after the pets. Camelia went with him, too, and they both shared a smile when they saw the cat and puppy had found a new chair in the study to curl up on, with a direct patch of sunlight warming them through the window. They retreated quietly from the room to let the animals rest. Raaz turned to Camelia.

"*Raspberry*?" Camelia asked, not even bothering to hide the surprised amusement that had broken through her melancholy.

"Ah, well, yes. It's a temporary placeholder, really," he said, lifting a shoulder. "Perhaps the pup got lost in the storm. We'll keep her until someone claims her. You named all the other animals, so I wanted the chance to name one, and it seems I've developed quite a weakness for whimsy as of late."

As well as a fondness for this place. And an attachment to a dog he would doubtless dote on even as he insisted he would never spoil her. Just as he denied he had a sweet tooth, though everyone in the Bay knew it by now and tried to ply him with pastries and cakes each time he visited the shops.

Camelia could picture it all. Raaz would treat this pup like a princess because she had almost drowned, and he would keep her as a lapdog. He would have to get another Scotch collie for actually herding the sheep, and would name that new dog *Pepper*, if his drawings were any indication. She realized the name for the pup she hadn't been able to read must have been *Raspberry*.

It hurt too much to see these visions of a life she wouldn't share with him.

"I really should be going to the inn," Camelia said, taking a step back from him. "I promised Binita I'd help with some final baking and preparations for the festival." She hesitated. "I might need to stay there for a night or two."

Camelia avoided looking at the duke's cognac eyes too closely, but she couldn't help noticing a slight stiffening in his posture.

The pause before he responded lasted too long. "Of course," he said briskly. "I understand."

"You may stay here," Camelia said, and then she winced. She hoped it didn't seem like she was giving Raaz an order. "If you wish to stay here, that is. But when I reach the inn, I can ask Kabir to check on the animals if you need to meet with the tenants again."

"Thank you, but that's not necessary," Raaz said. "I will manage. First, I'm going to ask around and determine if Raspberry escaped from any of the tenants' homes to try and reunite her with her rightful owner."

"That's a fine idea," Camelia said, before turning and striding away.

"Camelia," Raaz called out behind her.

She paused and looked over her shoulder. That forlorn expression once again shadowed his face, momentarily softening her resolve. "Yes, Raaz?"

"Is something the matter? Did I do something to earn your ire?"

He had done nothing. It was she who had been foolish enough to wish for more than he could give her. But she couldn't reveal her desires to him and burden him with that guilt. She was the one who needed to pull herself back into the boundaries they'd created, not him.

"No, Your Grace. Nothing you've done was wrong." The words felt unbearably final, and all she could do was leave him there in the hallway to retreat to her room and pack a small valise for the inn.

Of course he would attempt to find the pup's owner instead of claiming her as his own right away. Her heart squeezed at the thought of the duke being separated from the dog he'd so lovingly rescued. When she was finally ready to depart from the cottage, she tried to ignore the way every fiber of her being protested. Raaz did not come to watch her leave, nor did he ask her to stay. Everything felt so wrong, and Camelia didn't understand why, or how to fix it. She willed herself not to look back as she walked to the inn.

RAAZ SPENT THE EVENING ALTERNATING BETWEEN reading and pacing in the library. His chai had grown cold, and though his stomach growled, he didn't have the first clue about what he was going to eat tonight. There were some items still left in the larder, he supposed. He couldn't very well venture to the inn while Camelia was there, not when she wanted to be away from him. He didn't understand how their perfect day could have taken such a wrong turn. One minute they had been laughing by the pond, and the next, Camelia was asking for distance and time. To be sure, she had said it was to help prepare for the festival, but Raaz sensed there was more. He had combed through his words and actions, trying to make sense of it, to no avail.

Well, he wasn't going to refuse her or push. She had to sort through her thoughts and feelings on her own and make the decision to return to him on her own, too. Or not return to him. He tried not to think about that.

The most he could do was wait. Like he was some lovesick puppy.

Raaz shook his head with irritation and went to find Raspberry. The dog and cat had found a new spot to nap in a nook between the shelves.

"Please forgive me for saying I was going to try and seek out someone who wants you more," Raaz said to the pup as he picked her up and cradled her. "I've no intention of giving you up, but she'd probably think me a fool for waiting around here, hoping she'll realize she loves me as I love her."

Raspberry, of course, did little more than bark, but he appreciated it all the same. Billi, having been awoken by the commotion, yawned, found a new comfortable position, and went back to sleep. Raaz sighed. He ought to feed the animals —and himself—before turning in for the night. There was little else he could do now.

CHAPTER 22

Neither Binita nor Kabir questioned her when Camelia asked for a room at the inn for the night. In the morning, they welcomed the extra set of hands with only two days remaining before the festival, and Camelia relished the work. All the baking and cleaning kept her mind busy and her thoughts far from the duke.

Beside Camelia at the counter, Binita dragged a hand across her brow, swiping some errant flour over her tan skin. She tucked a strand of her greying dark hair back into the tight knot she wore when working. "We've been working without rest all day, but it still feels like there's so much to do."

"We'll manage to get it all done, and all those new visitors will be good for business," Camelia reassured the older woman.

"You're right, of course," Binita said. "I should focus on that. It will be good for the inn and the Bay as well. Every year I fret, and every year, just the same, it's all grand in the end."

But Camelia caught the weariness behind Binita's words, despite the older woman's attempt to present otherwise.

"Why don't you take a seat? Rest your feet for a while, and

tell me what I can do to make it easier for you," Camelia said, steering Binita out from behind the bar and into one of the chairs in the main dining area. "I'm certain you rose before the sun to begin baking."

"You've already been such a help," Binita said, "and while you have your new home to work on, at that. The cottage looks lovely, dear."

Binita stood after only a few minutes of idling. Camelia laughed and shook her head as the older woman started straightening the chairs and tables in the dining room. They would start preparing for the inn's evening guests soon.

"Thank you. We should be able to complete the stable roof repairs by the end of the week," Camelia said.

Binita turned to face her. "It seems as though the duke is still happy with the arrangement."

For one wild moment, Camelia thought she was referring to the deal of desires, and she gaped at the woman. She snapped her mouth shut when she realized Binita must mean the duke's management of the repairs. Of course that was all she could mean.

Binita smiled innocently. "We've set aside the raspberry galette your duke likes so much. Be a dear and bring it home to him."

Camelia's mouth fell open again. He wasn't *her* duke, and the implication that it was *their* home was too bold. But before Camelia could protest, their conversation was cut short as groups of people entered the inn. Serving everyone food and drink for the evening meal service kept Binita and Camelia busy, and by the time Camelia had a chance to catch her breath, she could do little more than drop into bed, exhausted from the day's work.

Tired as she was, sleep did not come easily. Camelia tossed and turned, wishing that she didn't know it was because she'd be more comfortable at home, in the cottage, in her own bed.

Sleeping next to Raaz. Their day at the lake had shown her what every day might be like with him, and she could see it even now, in the darkness behind her eyelids. No matter how tightly she squeezed her eyes shut, she could not stop her dreams. How happy she'd be with him.

Binita's words earlier that day hadn't helped. The people of the Bay had welcomed Raaz as if he'd lived here for years, in no small part because Raaz was so kind and generous, Camelia was sure. It made it all too easy to imagine a future where the duke really did live here. With her.

She forced herself to remember what she'd read. *I wonder what they will think . . .*

The words didn't hurt quite as much as they had in the library, not after Binita's shocking certainty. She waited for the usual excuses to come to her, how Raaz would have to leave for London, and how there was no use in asking him to stay. But as the dawn's new light began to brighten the sky, new thoughts intruded, and new questions emerged.

How could she imagine their life so clearly if it wasn't meant for her? How did it feel so natural to be with him, if he wasn't meant for her?

But she had felt this way before. Twice. And *meant to be* hadn't meant a thing, then.

Camelia swallowed past the knot in her throat. God, she wanted to trust this time could be different. But simply wanting would not make it so. There were only two choices. She could either step out of the duke's path to happiness, or ask Wednesbury outright if his path led to her as much as she believed her path led straight to him.

Neither choice guaranteed her heart would not be broken. Neither choice guaranteed a path without pain or regret. But that was what it took to love someone—the courage to choose them, to try, to trust, to communicate. To ask someone to stay.

I like *that you go after what you want—that you take risks.* That was what Raaz had said to her. Though the lord in London had humiliated her, that did not mean it had been wrong to speak openly of her love.

Knowing it was almost time to rise, Camelia dozed fitfully, a decision taking firmer root in her mind.

"I MUST RETURN TO THE COTTAGE BEFORE THE festival begins," Camelia announced to Binita and Kabir the following morning, after she'd washed and changed into fresh clothes. She held her valise with both hands.

Binita's eyes searched hers, but if the older woman noticed how tired Camelia was, she did not mention it. She said nothing of the fact that Camelia did not call the cottage *home*, either. "Of course, dear. Take as much time as you need."

"Thank you for the extra help," Kabir added. "I'm not sure we could have prepared all the food in time without you."

"It was my pleasure to help," Camelia said. "I'll meet you at our tables in the morning."

With every step away from the inn, she was closer to running, eager to return home, eager to tell the duke she wanted to try to open her heart again.

Camelia didn't see him outside when she neared the cottage. She unlocked the door and set off in search of Raaz. She found him in the library.

Of course. She might have known to check here first. He was reading and taking notes with dedicated focus, and he was wearing those endearing spectacles.

"You own so many books," Camelia said, stepping through the doorway and approaching the duke. She eyed the volumes lined up neatly on the library's shelves, as well as the tomes lying open and scattered across the desk. When the

163

duke's trunks had arrived at her cottage, most were taken directly to this room, as they were filled entirely with books. Only a few were upstairs in the bedroom with his clothes.

Raaz looked up in surprise. She saw a flash of what looked like genuine joy light his lovely cognac eyes, but then they dimmed. "You're here," he said, and it was a measured response. She deserved that. He must be unsure if she would stay.

"I finished helping Binita with the baking."

"I see," Raaz said.

Camelia loathed that he was now guarded with her and that she was the reason for his caution.

"As for the books, I only brought what was necessary," the duke said with a frown. "For my work."

Exasperated amusement interrupted her darkening mood. "All of these," Camelia said, gesturing to the numerous books along the library shelves for emphasis, "are for your work?"

"Yes," the duke insisted, crossing his arms. "Many are about legal and finance matters relevant to ducal estates. Some are about mathematics. Some on the study of botany. A few on art. And the others are to make sure my eyes don't glaze over from all the work required of learning about the first odious subject."

"Fine." Camelia laughed and held up her hands in surrender. "I can tell I've broached a delicate matter, and it's best if I retreat without saying more."

"I am the son of a duke who fancied himself a scholar." Raaz rolled his eyes and gave an elegant shrug. "And a man must have his hobbies. I don't see why it should be any different for a duke. In fact, I say that goes double for dukes— as most things do. We are, after all, supposed to live our lives in pursuit of leisure, not labor, are we not?"

All the duke had been doing since he arrived in the Bay was trying to make himself useful, but she refrained from pointing that out. "So, if you'd brought all the unnecessary books, too, what then? Would every shelf in my cottage be completely filled?" Camelia asked.

"No books are unnecessary," Raaz quickly corrected. "But yes, if I'd brought all of mine, then there would not be all these empty shelves."

"Raaz, please do be serious," Camelia said. "There is only one single bookcase in this entire library that is currently empty. That hardly justifies the word *all*."

"Fine," he said with a laugh. "Aren't you glad I only brought the ones needed for my work? If I'd brought all the rest of mine, then there would be no room for your books, too."

Camelia's laughter faded with this last statement, and she met his gaze.

It was time to try, whether or not her desires would be reciprocated.

"And is that what you want, Your Grace? To fill this library with both our books?"

Even as her heart raced with anticipation, a weight lifted from her shoulders. There was something liberating in letting herself want what she wished and voicing it aloud, too.

He was serious, too, now. "If that is what you desire."

"That is not an answer, Duke," Camelia said. "I asked you first, and this is my cottage."

One corner of his mouth tugged into a crooked smile at the reminder of their first meeting here. "Somehow, you always come first, which is, of course, how it should be."

"I agree, but I also simply like to win," Camelia said with a laugh. "Now, answer the question, if you please."

Raaz rose from the desk and strode to her. He tipped her chin up so their gazes met. He brushed his thumb along the line of her cheek. "Yes, I want to stay," he said in a fierce whisper.

Hope soared in Camelia's chest, but she needed to be sure. She turned into his touch and pressed a kiss to the center of his palm. When she met his gaze, she saw that his eyes were shining with unspoken emotion.

"Tell me more, Raaz," she whispered, too. "Tell me you're certain."

"I want to live here, in Robin Hood's Bay. With you. In this cottage," he said. "Forever, if you'll have me."

Camelia's breast felt tight, like it might burst, like she wasn't built to contain all this emotion that she wanted so much. Tears threatened, but she blinked rapidly to make sure she could get the rest of her words out. "I have to admit that I was wrong," she said. The shock in Raaz's face pleased the mischievous part of her. "First, I'm sorry I left for the inn. And second, I should have known one week of pleasure between us was never going to be enough."

"To be very clear, Camelia," Raaz said, eyes narrowed, "I'm well past the point of asking for more time together. I'm telling you I love you, and I'm asking you to marry me. Letting you leave for the inn without understanding what was wrong or how to help—without going after you when I knew you needed the time and space to sort through matters on your own—" He swallowed. "It was one of the hardest things I've ever done, Camelia. I thought I might have lost you. If marriage is not what you seek, I would understand, but don't let the past or our stations be what keeps us apart."

"I won't," Camelia said. "I promise I won't, Raaz. I want to stay." She swiped at the tears that filled her eyes. "You know, I was only too foolish to accept it until now, but I think I fell a little bit in love with you the minute you pulled out your penknife to slice an apple for Bakri."

Raaz's cognac eyes softened, nearly glowing with the same emotion that brimmed and burned within her. "Only a little?" He whispered. "Liar." Raaz pulled her closer to him and brushed a kiss against her temple. "Oh, my love, please don't cry. It kills me to see your tears."

She turned into him, steadying herself with the orange, almond, and bergamot scent of him and the soft lawn of his shirt that she was presently soaking with her tears. "And then I fell further when you organized the village assembly but didn't want anyone to know it was your idea," she said. She pulled back in the duke's embrace to look into his eyes. "There were countless other points in between, and I see now they were all along the same path. To you. Perhaps I'm not falling, just going the way I was always meant to go." Her voice softened. "To find you."

She hadn't hit the ground yet. And yes, it was possible that she wasn't done falling.

Or perhaps, it could also be that he hadn't let her down yet, and never would.

Maybe he would always be there to catch her.

If he loved her as much as she loved him.

There was only one way to find out. She had to choose. She had to let go of the past. She had to leap.

"You still haven't said if you'll be my wife," Raaz said, dragging a hand across the back of his neck. "Do you want me on one knee—would that help?"

"No," Camelia said.

"No?"

"Two knees will work better, I think," she said with a coy tilt of her head. "In fact, I think you'd best stay there for a while, Duke."

His eyes shone with forestalled tears. "Your wish is my command, Duchess." He laughed and tugged her close, cradling her jaw in both hands before lowering his lips to hers.

"I love you," Camelia said just before he kissed her. "I love you, I love you, I love you," she said in between kisses, to make certain he knew how much she meant it.

∼

AFTER THEY'D BOTH DRIED THEIR TEARS, RAAZ LED Camelia to the sofa, stunned that this shining sun of a woman was to be his. "Well, if we're to share our books, then I think we should discuss what you like to read," he said.

"I agreed to combine our books in this cottage's library," she teased, "not to share my books with you."

"And why not?" he asked.

"Because, Your Grace," she said. "The stories I like to read are not the most proper."

His brows lifted. "Now I'm well and truly intrigued, Miss Parikh," he said, "and you must tell me more."

"I could tell you," Camelia said, angling her head. "Or I could show you. The choice is yours, Duke."

"I prefer you show me what prurient things you've learned. But not here in the library," Raaz said. "I want you upstairs, in a bed. All to myself and with the door locked. No animals or distractions to think about."

"I see," Camelia whispered.

"I've wanted you in our bed since that first night we played vingt-et-un," he continued, in case she didn't understand that this was real for him. This was forever. "Besides, we don't have the space here to do the things I want to do with you."

"Oh? And what do you want to do with me?" she asked.

"I'll show you that, too, my clever girl," he said, taking her hand and interlacing their fingers. "Any objections?"

"Yes," she breathed.

"Yes?" he said. "You do have objections?"

"Oh, then I mean no," Camelia laughed. "No, I think that sounds rather perfect. Forgive me, I'm rather tired. I couldn't sleep a wink without you beside me."

"I felt the same," Raaz said, kissing her lips before he

swung her up into his arms and bounded up the stairs to her bedroom.

He laid her on the bed and collapsed beside her. "If you'd rather rest, we can do that."

"Later," she said with a smile. "But thank you. Now, just remember you asked for this." Her words reminded him of the first night they had kissed in this very room while playing cards.

"Go on," he said. Oh, he would remember. He planned on never forgetting a single detail of his time with her in this cottage, for as long as he lived. "Teach me about these wicked books you've devoured."

Camelia hesitated.

"Don't be shy now, sweetheart," Raaz encouraged in a soft tone. "I promise you're safe with me. You don't have to do anything you don't want to do, and I won't judge you for anything I have the privilege of sharing with you."

Camelia nodded and sat at the head of the bed, supported by pillows behind her. At the foot of the bed, Raaz lay on his side and propped his head up with one elbow.

They faced each other. And he waited for her to begin.

"The hero and heroine were both sculptors," Camelia said. "In Jaipur."

"I see," Raaz said, watching as she lifted her skirts, baring her supple legs to him one bronzed inch at a time. "And what next?"

"The story starts at the palace," Camelia said. "The characters were in competition for the Maharaja's patronage."

"Suspenseful," Raaz said.

Camelia draped her skirts over one arm and slid her hand between her thighs. Her fingers slipped between her dark curls and parted her folds. Her quim was already slick with arousal, glistening, beckoning for him to taste. God, how he wanted to lick her until not a drop of dew remained. And then he

SRI SAVITA

wanted to make her wet for him again. He wanted her soaked for him, squeezing his fingers and then his—

"Indeed, it was very intriguing. The story places an emphasis on hands and touch," Camelia said, interrupting his overeager musings. "Because of their preferred art form and skills with sculpting."

"I see," Raaz said, swallowing because his throat had gone dry. "Tell me more."

"Only if you touch yourself, too, Duke," she said in a throaty rasp that made his cock throb inside his trousers.

He tore his eyes away from her fingers circling her clitoris and slowly moved his gaze up to meet hers.

She smiled and stopped moving her fingers.

Raaz swallowed thickly. "Fine," he said. The word was a dark, guttural scrape of sound.

He opened the fall of his trousers. Camelia's gaze darted from his eyes to his lap. When she wet her lips, his cock twitched again. Gripping himself with a tight fist, Raaz began to fuck his own hand.

"What else?" he asked, straining to get the two small words out in between harsh breaths.

"He gave her a gift that he made," Camelia said, as she resumed touching herself. Her eyes moved from his face to his hand on his shaft, and then she tipped her head back, exposing the column of her throat to him.

"Focus on me, Camelia," Raaz said. "Don't come until you finish the story. What was the gift?"

"It was a toy," she said, meeting his gaze again. "Crafted from jade and sculpted to look like—" Her words broke off as she sighed and swallowed.

"Go on," Raaz said, and his voice came out husky.

"His cock," she said.

Raaz shuddered as she said the words. "And what did she do with the dildo?"

Camelia's breathing grew more rapid and shallow, and she moaned as she slipped two fingers inside her quim.

"What did she do with the jade, darling? Don't make me ask again," Raaz warned, in a voice that was more growl than words. "You started this game. You must finish it—before you can finish."

"She slid it inside her cunt," she whispered, "and pleasured herself."

That coarse word on Camelia's tongue was too much to bear, and he tore his hand away from his cock. "What in the— *Fuck*. You win. Fucking hell, I can't take it anymore." Raaz climbed forward on the bed. "I need to be inside you, Camelia. You're killing me."

She laughed, and he stole the sparkling sound from her lips, tangling his tongue with hers in a lazy glide. He drew back to rip off his shirt and trousers with as much grace as he could muster. After tossing his clothes to the carpet, he helped her with her dress, shift, and stays. He folded her garments neatly and placed them on the striped settee at the foot of the bed.

"Camelia," he said, wishing his fingers weren't trembling with his intense need for her. "I want to spend myself inside you, and then I want to do it again. All night. But tell me now if you don't want that, too."

"I want that," she whispered, laying back against the pillows and reaching for him. "Very much." Her hands tangled in his hair, and she pulled his face to hers.

He kissed her, then broke away with a short laugh. "God, I want this to be so good for you, darling."

"It will be," she reassured him.

His heart melted. Her earnest confidence was so endearing, and his pride didn't mind the stroking, either.

"But as much as I want to go slow," he continued, "sweetheart, I don't think I can. I fear it might be too much for me to manage at present." He'd been waiting an eternity to enter her, after all.

A slow, sly smile bloomed on her face. "Then don't."

Damn. Those words in that vixen-like voice, well, it was enough to unman him right now. Almost. But he gritted his teeth and recovered his restraint.

"I will still make it good," he promised her.

Raaz kissed her forehead, her temple, her closed eyelids, and her cheeks. He dragged his mouth and tongue along the underside of her jaw, down her neck, and across Camelia's collarbone. His lips closed around the stiff peak of one nipple and then the other, as he teased her with his teeth and tongue. He traced a path along the curve of her waist, lightly biting her there before sliding lower to settle between her legs. Raaz could resist for a little while longer to make sure she was truly ready for him.

"Raaz, stop," Camelia whined, clutching his shoulders and trying desperately to drag him back up to her.

"What is it?" he asked. The scent of her was so alluring, it made him salivate with hunger.

"You promised you weren't going to take your time," she said.

CHAPTER 23

"I never said I wouldn't take my time. I said I couldn't go slow once I'm inside you. There's a difference." Raaz laughed. "Don't you want me to taste you?"

"No—that is, yes, obviously, of course. But not right now, another time." She stumbled through the words, trying to articulate how much the acute heat of lust was driving her wild and addling her thoughts and words. "I can't wait—I want you too much."

She could tell it was her last sentence that snapped the fragile remaining threads of his restraint. His cognac eyes brimmed with brightly burning desire, and he brought the head of his cock to notch at her center. Camelia nodded, and he slid into her inch by inch. She gasped and whimpered until he was seated to the hilt. She felt full in the very best way, and she rolled her hips against him, urging him to give her more. "Raaz. Please."

"Fuck, Camelia," he groaned. "You're so warm and wet and soft, I—" His words broke off as he grimaced.

"Don't hold back, Raaz," she said, placing a hand against his cheek. "I can take it. All of you."

She could tell they were the right words to say—that all he'd wanted was the reassurance he wouldn't hurt or break her before he truly unleashed himself. Raaz pulled back and slid in again, slowly stretching her as he built momentum. "More," she said. "Give me more of you."

And he did then, driving into her with hard thrusts. Camelia tried to focus on every sensation inside and around her. Every sound Raaz made. The scent of his skin. The touch of his hands as he made sure she was all right the entire time. The agony in his face from how long he had waited and how much he wanted this, too.

"Let go," she whispered. It was as much a romantic command as it was a reminder. She said the words for him as much as she did for herself.

Her release was sudden and spiraled through her with a rush of heat. Camelia's muscles clenched around Raaz in hard, greedy pulses and then relaxed as pleasure washed through her in an unending cascade. The duke followed close behind, tightening his hold on her as he shuddered and groaned. After finishing inside her, he collapsed against her. He closed his eyes, and when his breathing had slowed, he rolled to the side and fell back against the pillows.

They stayed in the blissful aftermath of lovemaking for only a moment. Raaz soon stood to fetch the basin and ewer of water from the dressing table, then toweling to clean Camelia first, himself second. He gently wiped the warm cloth between her legs and across the soft skin of her stomach.

"Next time, you can read me that tale in its entirety, and then we'll buy every other naughty book you've enjoyed and fill the remaining shelves in our library," Raaz said with a grin.

Camelia laughed, loving the promise in that little word, *our*. The duke stole the sound from her lips with a kiss.

This time when they made love, it was languorous, with fits of laughter as they twisted and tangled in the sheets. They stayed there like that under the blankets until the sun went down. When Raaz's breathing grew slow and even, Camelia closed her eyes, too, feeling safe, warm, and at peace beside him.

∼

RAAZ WOKE IN THE MORNING WITH A CRUSHING feeling in his chest. Something heavy weighed on his heart. Opening his eyes with a resigned sigh, Raaz was greeted by a pair of golden feline ones staring directly at him. He laughed. "How the hell did you get in here, Billi?"

He scratched the cat under its chin and behind its ears until his efforts were rewarded with happy purring. Raaz moved Billi off his chest so he could sit up. He turned to Camelia's side of the bed, but she wasn't there. The bedroom door was left ajar, which explained how the cat had found him. Raaz frowned. She must've risen early to set up for the festival, because her clothes from last night were still where he had folded them on the settee.

Raaz stood and stretched with a groan before folding the coverlet back. Throwing on his banyan, he retrieved his shirt and trousers, still scattered on the carpet.

"Come, let's find the others," he said to the sleeping cat. "I'm sure everyone is eager for breakfast. You can have your nap later."

Raaz stepped behind the screen to change. He scooped up the cat and dashed down the stairs. After feeding Billi and Raspberry some cooked chicken, Raaz went outside to muck out Shandar, Pavan, and Bakri's stalls and feed them as well. Once all the animals were taken care of, Raaz ran back inside to wash and change into fresh clothes.

He settled into the desk in the library with a tea tray loaded with chai, raspberry jam, and bread. After he drank a cup of chai, Raaz's attention landed on his journal. Something poked out from between the pages. He flipped the book open, and there lay a card.

It was painted to look like the Queen of Hearts, but the woman in the portrait was unmistakably Camelia.

Raaz quickly turned the card over. On the back of the card in her neat penmanship were the words, *Fate or choice. It does not matter how we found each other. For me, you are both.* Raaz stared at the elegant script. This had to be why she had looked at his open journal the other day when he was asleep.

Raaz reread the pages that Camelia had slipped the portrait card between. They detailed some of his more personal desires, rather than simply documenting their work on the cottage and meetings with the tenants. She'd seen his wishes for his mother and siblings, as well as his yearning for a wife and children of his own. For Camelia to be that wife.

Except, if she had read all of that, she wouldn't have been so uncertain of his intentions yesterday. He frowned and reread his words, trying to imagine any of the lines taken out of context. Worry needled at him. What, exactly, had she read? Had this been what made her leave for the inn that night?

He stood and tucked the journal under his arm. They had not discussed this, and he had to make sure she knew everything. He'd wanted her from the very start, as she had the day he sliced the first apple for Bakri. She *was* his desire. Everything he'd written on these pages was about her. He wanted to share his life with her, their animals, everything they had built together in the Bay.

Their home.

CHAPTER 24

"GOOD MORNING, YOUR GRACE," A VOICE SAID FROM behind him as he passed The Bay Blossom.

Raaz turned to see Binita standing a few paces away, appearing to have just exited the inn. "Good morning, Binita. I'm looking for Camelia."

"She's at the festival." The older woman pointed down the hill to where what seemed to be the whole village was already gathered in the streets. Shops had set up tables in front of their doors piled high with food, drink, and wares for sale. "I came back to the inn to retrieve the extra pastries I need to take down to The Bay Blossom's table," Binita said.

"Let me help," Raaz offered, following her inside the shop. He took one of the baskets from her hands, all the while fighting to ignore the tempting, sweet aroma of raspberries that wafted toward him from the assorted baked confections inside.

"Come on then, Your Grace," Binita said, leading the way. "Let's go make your grand entrance."

"Well, well, well. Look who decided to join us," Leo said when Raaz approached The Bay Blossom's table. He snatched a raspberry pastry from the basket before Raaz could swat his friend's hand away. It didn't help that Raaz was still encumbered by the journal under his arm.

"Oh, I don't think Wednesday's here to see us," Percy said, also dodging Raaz easily to take a small raspberry galette. Percy tipped his chin to where Camelia stood with Kabir and a group of children.

"You'll have to pay for those treats, you know," Raaz said to Leo and Percy.

"Binita said we didn't," Leo said.

"Because you'd pay for them," Percy added.

"Fine," Raaz agreed with a sigh.

"Go on, then," Leo said, before biting into his pastry.

"Good luck," Percy added. "We'll be here if you need a tart to comfort you later."

Raaz rolled his eyes. His friends didn't know Camelia had already agreed to marry him and become his wife and his duchess. He just wanted her to know he'd wanted this for longer than only these last few days—that he didn't just want a wife, but for her to be that wife.

He approached Kabir and Camelia. She was helping Kabir organize the children who wanted to fly kites.

"There you are," Camelia said.

"Here I am," Raaz said. He was about to ask Camelia if they could go somewhere quieter to talk when Kabir turned to Raaz with a smile.

"Ah, Your Grace, how kind of you to help." He handed Raaz a stack of kites. "Would you and Camelia pass these out to the children? I'm going to make sure the youngest ones don't get too tangled up in the spools of string to have any fun."

"I—uh," Raaz started, but the older man had already turned away to chase after two children who were running toward the beach.

"Will you help me fly a kite, Your Grace?"

Raaz turned and gazed down. A young girl looked up at Raaz with large, dark eyes, and his chest was too tight to say the words to refuse her. So he only nodded.

"My name is Nadeen. I'm five years old," she said, and then she took him by the hand and walked toward the hill where the other children were gathering.

"I see you've made a friend, Duke," Camelia said with a smile, as they passed out kites to the children.

"It is rather easy to do when you grew up with four younger siblings," Raaz said dryly, but he couldn't stop himself from smiling, too.

"I trust you slept well?" Camelia asked in a low murmur, and her amber eyes sparkled in the sunlight.

Raaz was about to answer his teasing duchess-to-be, but Kabir interrupted them.

"Thank you both," he said. "Binita and I can take it from here. You two should go enjoy yourselves. It's your first time seeing all the festivities in the Bay."

"If you're sure," Raaz said.

"We're sure," Binita told him with a knowing smile.

"Thank you," Camelia said with a wave.

When they'd walked far enough away from the music and dancing, Raaz pulled her to his chest in a fierce embrace.

"God, I love you," Raaz murmured against her hair.

Camelia melted against him, and Raaz had to resist letting slip one of the hopelessly foolish and flowery names he'd taken to calling his future wife in his head over these past few whimsy-filled weeks. Endearments like *my light* and *sunray*. *Sunbeam*, *sunflower*, and *sunshine goddess*.

She pulled back and pressed a finger to the furrow between his brows. "Raaz, is something the matter?"

"Nothing's wrong," he assured her. He took her hand, and they walked toward the shade of a large tree on a more secluded hill. Its canopy hid them from view—not that there was anyone around to witness their whispers and laughs with the festival still fully underway.

"I read the note on the back of your card," Raaz said. "It's a beautiful portrait, by the way. I should like to see the one you painted of me as well."

"How do you know there is one I painted of you, Your Grace?" Camelia teased.

Raaz slid her a look. "Well, where else am I supposed to write you a love note of my own?"

Camelia smiled, but then glanced at the journal he held and grew somber. "I read more than I meant to," she admitted.

"I know," Raaz said, sitting on the ground and pulling her onto his lap. "But you may have also stopped reading too soon. You should know everything I ever wished for was you. The life I wrote about—that's the life I want with you, our animals, this village, and our home. I've been thinking of you as my wife for days. Absolutely, on the day we spent by the pond." He hesitated, willing his face not to heat. "And certainly, when I plaited your hair after our bath." He opened the journal to the right page and held it out, then reread his own words as she studied the page.

I wonder what they will think of me finding the woman I love in the place my father loved. There's a poetic symmetry to it. A rightness. A balance. They were right to send me to Robin Hood's Bay. Or maybe it was my father watching from above who guided me here. Perhaps she was the one who called me here. However it happened, I'm glad it did, and I don't ever want to leave here. Or Camelia. Especially not her.

"Oh, my love," Camelia said. She looked up, and tears

shone in her eyes. She pressed a palm to his cheek. "You're sweet to tell me. But any hesitation on my part was due to my own doubts about myself, never about you."

"Good," Raaz said, turning his face into her touch and kissing the center of her palm. "For a moment I was worried you didn't know how much I want you—how perfect I find you. I didn't want to overwhelm you the night you left for the inn, but I'm concerned you left because I withheld the true depth of my desire for you."

"I love that you gave me the time and space to decide for myself," Camelia assured him. "And I love you." She kissed his cheek. "Always." She kissed the other cheek. "Forever."

He brought his lips to hers for another kiss.

"Someone will see us," Camelia whispered with a laugh.

"There's no one here," Raaz murmured. "Everyone else is still at the festival."

Camelia turned to straddle his lap, and he angled his mouth over hers again. She twined her arms around his neck as his warm hands reached under her dress to pull her hips closer to him. Her movements were hidden by her skirts as she freed Raaz's cock from his trousers and slowly sank down, letting his length and girth stretch and fill her, until they began to move together. Camelia draped her skirts over his arm to preserve some semblance of modesty, though only nature was witness to their love, and she was sure it would not judge. After all, what they were doing *was* natural, animal in its purest form.

As they made love, she and Raaz traded whispered plans and promises. Camelia tried not to melt at his words, but every time he said her name, it was so tender and sweet, and there was so much love there. She trusted him, *and* she wanted him. That was more than she'd ever found all in one man. Soon her breaths grew rapid, and she gasped, taking one more deep lungful of air before falling under the surface, sinking into the waves of pleasure that cascaded through her. He tumbled after her into bliss. Camelia braced her hands on the tree trunk that Raaz's back rested against—neither one of them knowing they created a new branch to the Wednesbury line that very day.

CAMELIA AND RAAZ WERE MARRIED IN THE LAST long golden days of summer. Camelia's parents—whose voyage Raaz had happily paid for—Raaz's mother, his four younger siblings, their friends from London, and the entire Bay were in attendance. They held the wedding outdoors at their cottage. The weather was beautiful—not a single cloud was in the blue sky that day in the Bay. Soon after, the Duke and Duchess of Wednesbury began their married life together by writing and illustrating the children's story ideas Raaz had documented in his journal. They began, of course, with Basil's tale.

The following year, when the first buds bloomed, Raaz and Camelia welcomed their son and heir, Tarun, into the world. He was named in honor of Raaz's father, and their boy brought with him another beautiful spring to the beloved Bay.

EPILOGUE

ROBIN HOOD'S BAY, 1820

"THAT'S CROOKED AND OFF CENTER. A LITTLE MORE to the left," Leo said, and Raaz moved the plaque he was trying to hang.

"No, that's too far," Percy said. "A touch back to the right ought to do it."

Raaz sighed and stepped in the opposite direction. "How about now?"

"That's perfect, jaan," Camelia said.

"Yes, it looks wonderful, Wednesday," Leo agreed.

Raaz stepped back to admire the view with his wife and his friends.

"Pappa, what is that?" Raaz's two-year-old son, Tarun, who shared his name with Raaz's father, asked the question from where he stood next to Camelia, holding his mother's hand.

The duke lifted their child into his arms and walked closer to the plaque he and Camelia had repainted. Raaz pointed to each of the words on the sign. "This is Wednesday Cottage, beta, our home."

"Look who's finally made it," Percy said, as horses stopped outside the gate behind them.

Raaz turned and smiled when he saw his mother and siblings exit their carriages. Though they'd all moved to the Bay to be closer to him, Camelia, and their son, all of the Panchals still couldn't manage to get anywhere on time together. Raaz's other London friends had just arrived, too, and his son was excited to see Prashant Kaka and Aarav Kaka again.

"We're here, we're here," his mother said, dashing over and scooping her first grandchild from Raaz's arms to pepper his face with kisses, while Tarun giggled and told his ba about the gifts Leo Kaka and Percy Kaka brought him.

Raaz and Camelia greeted his siblings and their friends.

"I brought you toys and books as well," Raaz's mother told Tarun.

"There's no need to spoil the child," Raaz muttered to Camelia. They trailed behind while the rest of their family walked inside the cottage.

"My love, you know he's not just a child," Camelia said, and her amber gaze sparkled with mirth. "He's the heir."

"Not you, too, with all that stuff and nonsense," Raaz said, pulling his wife closer to kiss her temple.

"Your mother's only indulging in the duty of a grandmother," Camelia said with a laugh. "It's our responsibility to keep our son's pride in line."

"Yes, and it seems we'll have to toil diligently to counteract the efforts of every doting kaka, fia, uncle, aunty, ba, and bapuji. That's far too many people to track in the Bay alone, to say nothing of London and India. I fear our boy will become insufferable before he reaches the age of five."

"We certainly have our work cut out for us, but such are

the labors of parenthood," Camelia agreed, gazing up at him and smiling.

"How are you feeling?" Raaz asked her gently, resting his palm on her stomach.

"I'm fine," she said, stroking his cheek. "There's nothing to worry about, which is also what I said this morning when you asked me in bed."

Camelia's pregnancy and the birth of their son had been, on the whole, quite smooth, which was a tremendous blessing. He would be forever grateful to have a happy and healthy child with the woman he loved, and that Camelia had her strength and was well too. That his darling wife had survived childbirth and wanted another child with Raaz was not something he would ever take for granted. To share in their devotion to each other as spouses, and to see aspects of each of them in their precious son, was a beautiful gift. Learning how to parent together was an adventure in itself, and Camelia was the perfect partner to be on that journey with. Raaz would do anything for his son and Camelia, but he'd never want his beloved wife to feel any pressure to have children, much less create an heir, despite his own desires.

Somehow, even now that they had their son and an heir for the Wednesbury line, it did not decrease Raaz's worries over the upcoming birth of their second child. In fact, Raaz was only all too aware of everything he had to lose in this life —everything he couldn't grasp tightly to him at all moments of the day.

"You know, I don't believe it gets any easier," he said to Camelia, "letting your heart live outside of your body. There are only more pieces of it I have to keep a closer watch on."

"Did this only now dawn on you, Duke?" Camelia teased. "I thought the man I married was far wiser than that."

"No, Duchess," Raaz said with a smile. "I suppose I'm

simply saying it's nice to have so many people to care about, and who care about me in return."

She leaned her head against his shoulder. "Yes, my dear husband," his wife said, "it is very nice indeed to be so loved."

"Would you two please make haste?" Raaz's sister, Thanya, called to them from the doorway. "The rest of us have been ready to depart on this picnic for ages."

"It seems we're being summoned, Your Grace," Camelia said with a smile. She took Raaz's hand. He laced his fingers together with hers, and she tugged him toward the cottage—to this magical place that was their home in the Bay, to their family and friends, and toward their life together that was only just beginning.

THANYA'S FAMILY DID NOT, IN FACT, GO ON THIS picnic yet—not for another two whole hours. First her dear sweet tyrant of a nephew curled up on the sofa with the puppy and cat and asked his father to read him the story about *King Basil of the Bay*. Naturally, her brother could refuse his son nothing, and he obliged. Then her mother asked for a tour of the cottage from Camelia Bhabhi. Thanya's two younger sisters joined the tour as well, before they decided to borrow some of their sister-in-law's romantic novels and disappeared to read. Lastly, her other older brother was teaching Leo and Percy how to make chai for everyone while they waited to finally leave for this picnic.

"There's someone knocking at the door," Thanya called to Raaz, who was now reading the badger story for a second time before the little terror would allow his pappa to put the book away.

"Yes, thank you, Thanya. As you're no doubt aware, I'm busy at present with the delicate art of trying to avoid kindling a two-year-old's tantrum," her brother said dryly. "Will you please go see who it is?"

"Fine," Thanya said, since she was already standing. She left the drawing room and walked to the front door. She swung it wide open, planning to simply whirl away and be done with the matter. But it seemed her feet would not move, and somehow, she lost whatever clever words had been in her head a moment ago.

"Hello," the man standing in front of her said. "I'm the Duke of Ramsgate. Wednesbury invited me here today."

The Duke of Ramsgate, he said. This man, a duke? It seemed improbable. Well, at least in her eyes. Thanya had never seen a duke like this before. He was young, perhaps only a year or two older than she was, with a fine, fit figure she could appreciate—and she did, dragging her gaze down the long, lean lines of his body and back up to the angles of his face. It was clear he possessed an athletic grace even while standing still. His posture was perfect. And he was tall. So tall, in fact, that Thanya had to tip her head back to look into his liquid, dark eyes—like ink they were, those eyes. They were eyes she could drown in, were she not focused on the fact that they were fanned by the longest lashes she'd ever seen on a person.

His warm brown skin made it look as though he'd spent the entire morning swimming in the sun. And his rosy flush and tousled dark hair made it look like he'd spent the entire morning riding a horse—or being ridden in a lover's bed. Thanya couldn't be sure which was true, and so she took a step backward, startled that she was having such shocking thoughts about a stranger in the first place. Perhaps she'd been reading one too many of her sister-in-law's erotic novels. Or, more likely, it was because the Duke of Ramsgate was the most handsome—well, no, that wasn't the right word, really, *beautiful* was more like it—man she had ever seen.

187

Unfortunately, to make matters worse, the duke seemed to know very well what effect he had on people. A smug smile curved the line of his too-perfect mouth. Instantly, Thanya schooled her features into an expression of disinterest, not wanting to give him the satisfaction of being the reason she had taken leave of her senses. She preferred her men to be more humble than what she now saw in his face.

"Thanya?" Raaz said, coming up behind her in the hallway. "For heaven's sake, shut the door before Raspberry and Billi get out, and don't just stand there staring at the man. Let him pass."

"I-I wasn't staring." She blinked out of her daze and turned to her brother as she stepped out of the path of the two men.

Raaz shook his head and addressed the duke. "I'm sorry my sister was barring your entry, Ramsgate, but it's good to finally meet you in person. We don't stand on ceremony here, so please, come inside and make yourself comfortable."

"That's kind of you," the Duke of Ramsgate said, entering and taking in the surroundings. "You have a beautiful home."

"I appreciate that," Raaz said, closing the front door and beaming with pride. "I couldn't have done it without my duchess, of course."

"I look forward to meeting Her Grace," Ramsgate said. "Thank you for inviting me today."

"Of course, it's our pleasure. Now, besides enjoying a picnic with some of my friends and family, there is another reason I wrote you," her brother said, leading his new friend toward the drawing room. "I wanted to discuss a Wednesbury property that you might be interested in buying."

The men's chatter disappeared as they turned the corner, and Thanya realized she was still standing stunned in the hallway, alone with her shocking thoughts.

She slumped against the closed front door. God, she

would have to spend the whole afternoon with this hazardously handsome duke—and her family too, together, all at the same time. She closed her eyes, hoping she wouldn't say anything foolish, that her family wouldn't tell Ramsgate any silly stories about her, and that she'd survive the picnic with her pride intact.

Perhaps then she could figure out why this man affected her so much.

THANK YOU FOR READING!

Did you enjoy this book? As an independent author, I would be grateful if you left a rating and/or review on your ebook retailer website, Goodreads, StoryGraph, Instagram, or wherever else you talk about and share books on social media.

If you'd like exclusive access to the latest book news, project updates, bonus content, sneak peeks, and other writing fun, then join my author newsletter on Substack. Use the link or QR code below.

https://srisavita.substack.com/

AUTHOR'S NOTE

I've always gravitated toward writing and research, so it makes sense that I write historical romance. Specifically, I write stories set in the UK during (mostly) the Regency period, but I've also been writing some short stories set in the Victorian era. My strengths as an academic help with the research and writing, but the focus of my stories is Indian representation in romance. I would love to see more South Asian and Indian representation in all romance genres, but historical romance especially. Yes, of course, more stories set in historical India would be fantastic to read, and I am writing some myself, but a call for these stories should not confine Indian historical romance authors like me from writing about different parts of the world and periods.

I love reading stories set in the Regency period and writing within this era because there are many levers with which to create conflict, challenge, and change. But I don't endorse old-fashioned limitations. I want characters to dismantle, or redefine, those societal, class, and economic barriers. Of course, I also like the glamor and the tension unique to the time period, because I'm a romance and erotica author. Moreover, as a North American who has sometimes felt out of place in the country they were born and raised in, writing about Indian people navigating life in England holds additional appeal.

My goal with writing fiction is to create stories of hope and to have fun in the process, because I'm doing this first and foremost for myself—writing the kinds of stories I wish I could read. It is hard work, and above all, I want to be kind to and take care of my readers, characters, and myself with my words. And so, you'll find at times I walk alongside the path that history took, instead of directly on it. My characters must make their own way in Regency England, and so too, I've had to carve out space for my stories within this genre that I love so much. I will add, as strong encouragement, it should not be an impossible path to travel for readers. Courtney Milan said it best: "People of color are hidden in every Regency romance scene—in the tea, sugar, rum, silk, and cotton—and it is time to put them directly on the page, as something more than the product of their ill-gotten labor."

We've always existed in the backdrops of these stories, in the imported goods, on the table, and in the clothing. It's long past time for us to be the main characters. I write with that mission at the forefront of my mind. As I said before, the focus of my fiction is Indian representation in romance and erotica. One of the things I most enjoyed about writing *The Deed with the Duke* was finding ways to meld Indian culture with Regency society. When I learned that ballroom floors often had chalked floral and arabesque designs, I immediately thought of rangoli, and added that to the scene. So, any creative liberties I take are with deliberate care to ensure my characters' stories are not only centered on trauma. History, too, is a narrative, and it's important to remember whose hand held the pen.

I set my book in Robin Hood's Bay because of the village's history as a smuggling haven, which ties into some of my other works. Also, the real village of Robin Hood's Bay has a folk festival that was the inspiration for the start-of-summer festival included in my story. Regarding the cottage, I've long been enamored by the house as a character and had conversations about this with bookish friends of mine as well. It's an image that plays especially well in historical romance, and while the cottage orné in this story isn't a gothic figure, Wednesday Cottage still has a character all its own (and a few supporting actors in the form of adorable animals and their antics). I loved the idea of these intentionally picturesque (though perhaps a touch impractical) country homes with a pretty facade that might be hiding some flaws, much like Camelia and Raaz, and I would venture to say much like many of us as well. Before our heroine and hero can make this facsimile of a house into a home, they must first open up about their vulnerabilities to each other, overcome their fears, and work together—and I enjoy how getting the cottage in order maps onto the romantic arc. Camelia and Raaz were building a life together before they even knew they were—hence the themes of fate and choice in the book—and that was great fun to write.

When I read in my research that the cottage orné was sometimes a home for newly married couples, I had the idea of it being a special place for Raaz's parents, especially his father. Then Raaz's journey in inheriting the Wednesbury title involved falling in love with the village and cottage the same way his father did, and it involved Raaz finally making it a home for himself and Camelia when they marry. Grief and growth are themes for this story, and a lot of my writing. The cyclical nature of that character development, along with the image of a literal family tree, and mention of Raaz and Camelia's son in the epilogue, felt important to include. Stories about siblings are deeply significant to me; it's one of the longest relationships a person can have, and I lost my younger sister to cancer in 2020. I haven't grown up with the large family gatherings depicted in the media about holidays in the US, or large extended family gatherings depicted in the media about Indian families. So, I've written the Panchals to help bring an Indian community to the Regency era and have those large family dynamics play out in a controlled way on the page. I look forward to writing forthcoming happily-ever-afters for Raaz's four younger siblings (see Thanya's scene in the epilogue!), and I hope you'll continue to follow along and read as these characters turn over new leaves and put down roots in Robin Hood's Bay.

ACKNOWLEDGMENTS

There are many people who have helped me along the way in my writing journey. First, to my younger sister who is always in our hearts, I write because you helped me find my way back to reading for fun again. Somehow you always knew I could do this, even before I did. Love you always and miss you forever.

My infinite thanks to my family and friends for listening to my plot talks among other rants and rambles. Next, thank you to Dr. J. and Mischa Eliot for including me in the Cards of Passion project, and all my coauthors in this series. To my writing communities, and all my author friends, thank you for answering my questions and for making writing less lonely.

An extra note of gratitude for those who read about Camelia and Raaz in their earliest form: Nicole Pamukcu, Beth Wrisley, Katherine Grant, my editor, Kaitlin Schmidt, and my proofreader, Kelly at Velvet Library. Your feedback and encouragement helped me shape this story so it can truly shine, and I'm happy to have such supportive readers, writers, and friends in my corner. Thank you for cheering me on (and reminding me to be kind to and care for myself too). Another special thanks to Nicole, who planted the seed that grew into Basil the badger—the mammal, the myth, the legend. Thank you, friend, for the reminder to have fun while writing, and to make my stories exactly what I want them to be.

A note of love and appreciation for my cat, Leo, who stayed up with me many a late night while I wrote, revised, and rewrote, as well as the cats of the wonderful people in my life:

Percy, Blair, and Evie. The names of these three feline friends are used with permission (from their people) for characters in the Savita-verse.

To libraries and librarians, thank you for all you do to help nurture readers and writers everywhere. To the authors of all the books I've read and love, thank you, you inspired me to write my own. I am grateful to live in the age of the internet, and grateful to all the people writing about Regency era history, fashion, architecture, etc. out there, you all are amazing. Thank you for providing such a wealth of valuable knowledge and resources to help me craft my world and characters with authenticity.

And finally, to you, the reader, thank you for choosing this book, and I hope you enjoy your time visiting my characters in Robin Hood's Bay. Have a raspberry pastry while you're there, for me.

ABOUT THE SERIES

LIFE CAN CHANGE WITH THE DRAW OF A CARD.

When sex educator Liv Thornton created a transformative card deck of affirmations to help women embrace their sexuality and integrate that part of themselves into all that they are, she never expected her cards to find their way into so many women's stories.

Like the jeans in *The Sisterhood of the Traveling Pants*, those cards inserted themselves into the lives of a modern-day throuple playing with boundaries, a bold heroine in the Regency era, a warrior elf and his sinful liaison in a fantastical world, a befuddled small-town witch trying to keep her secret, a contemporary bookstore owner rewriting her self-image, a cartomancer who can taste desires, and more.

Readers can cross genres and time by reading the stand-alone stories in this series in any order. Watch for cameo appearances of select characters between stories.

In the real world, the Cards of Passion deck actually exists in physical and digital form. It's called Purple Passion Reflections for Women by Dr. J. Each author used the real deck to inspire the sexual journeys of their heroines and heroes.

Imagine how a deck of sexuality affirmations could alter your life. Follow the women's paths in these stories, then create your own real-world adventure.

The cards are at your fingertips.

Check out the books in the *Cards of Passion* series:

https://geni.us/CardsofPassionRomance
Physical edition of the deck:
https://geni.us/CardsofPassionp
Digital edition of the deck:
https://geni.us/CardsofPassiond

About the Author

Sri Savita is an award-winning romance author who loves writing about love, and she believes in the magic of a good story with heart, heat, hope, & happily ever after. Sri's work centers and celebrates Indian characters in romance with bold heroines, besotted heroes, and lyrical longing. You can learn more about her projects on her website: sri-savita.com. With a Ph.D. in Psychology, research is naturally part of the fun of crafting fiction for Sri, and she enjoys bringing her passion for learning, reading, language, and psychology to her characters and stories.

- amazon.com/author/sri-savita
- bookbub.com/authors/sri-savita
- goodreads.com/srihere
- srisavita.substack.com
- instagram.com/sri_writes_here
- pinterest.com/sri_writes_here
- facebook.com/sri.writes.here

Also by Sri Savita

CONTRIBUTOR

Best Women's Erotica of the Year, Volume 10